"It's not like I can get pregnant all over again."

"This is a bad idea."

"Probably," Nicole said with a fleeting smile that did strange things to his insides. "But at the moment I can't say I care. We're both adults, and given the situation, I think it's only natural that we've gotten…closer."

She took a deep breath, and for the first time Ethan saw a hint of nerves.

She exhaled and twined her fingers together beneath her robe. His job was to protect her, not take advantage of her. But how could he resist what she was offering? Especially when she said, "I want this. I really do." That was all it took.

JESSICA ANDERSEN

CLASSIFIED BABY

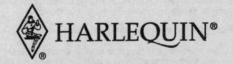

TORONTO • NEW YORK • LONDON
AMSTERDAM • PARIS • SYDNEY • HAMBURG
STOCKHOLM • ATHENS • TOKYO • MILAN • MADRID
PRAGUE • WARSAW • BUDAPEST • AUCKLAND

Special thanks and acknowledgment are given to Jessica Andersen for her contribution to the BODYGUARDS UNLIMITED, DENVER, CO miniseries.

To Joanna Wayne, Ann Voss Peterson, Elle James, Kathleen Long and Cassie Miles, for joining me in writing the six books of this series, and to Allison Lyons for conceiving these wonderful stories.

ISBN-13: 978-0-373-88779-8
ISBN-10: 0-373-88779-5

CLASSIFIED BABY

Copyright © 2007 by Harlequin Books S.A.

www.eHarlequin.com

Printed in U.S.A.

ABOUT THE AUTHOR

Though she's tried out professions ranging from cleaning sea lion cages to cloning glaucoma genes, from patent law to training horses, Jessica is happiest when she's combining all these interests with her first love: writing romances. These days she's delighted to be writing full-time on a farm in rural Connecticut that she shares with a small menagerie and a hero named Brian. She hopes you'll visit her at www.JessicaAndersen.com for info on upcoming books, contests and to say "hi!"

Books by Jessica Andersen

HARLEQUIN INTRIGUE
833—COVERT M.D.
850—THE SHERIFF'S DAUGHTER
868—BULLSEYE
893—RICOCHET*
911—AT CLOSE RANGE*
928—RAPID FIRE*
945—RED ALERT
964—UNDER THE MICROSCOPE
982—PRESCRIPTION: MAKEOVER
1005—CLASSIFIED BABY

*Bear Claw Creek Crime Lab

CAST OF CHARACTERS

Ethan Moore—A loner who freelances for Prescott Personal Security (PPS) as a bodyguard. Ethan doesn't consider himself part of the PPS team and has no intention of replacing the wife he lost years ago.

Nicole Benedict—When trouble with her biofuel project and ex-boyfriend drives her to cut loose for a night, Nic has no idea how much trouble she's going to wind up in, or how far she'll have to go to save the child she and Ethan conceive that night.

Robert Prescott—The ex-British intelligence founder of PPS has miraculously returned from the dead, only to find that things have changed while he was away. Now he's fighting for his life on one front, fighting for his marriage on another.

Evangeline Prescott—Robert's wife kept PPS running—and flourishing—while waiting for his return. Now that he's back, she refuses to let him take over the investigation that could end with both of their deaths.

Clive Fuentes—Robert's ex-mentor used him as a front for dirty business dealings, then tried to kill him when he got too close to the truth.

Stephen Turner—The head of media megacorporation Tri Corp. Media (TCM) seems clean, but if that's the case, why do so many of the clues lead back to TCM?

Olivia Turner—Robert's ex-wife, now married to the head of TCM, is an unhappy woman.

Chapter One

Colorado, USA

"I'm here to see Ethan Moore at Prescott Personal Securities." Nicole Benedict resisted the urge to wipe her damp palms on her jeans. The lobby of the posh Denver office building was cooler than the summer day outside, but the air-conditioning did little to quell her nervous jitters.

The uniformed guard tapped the touch pad on his computer screen, selecting the roster for PPS. "And you are?"

"Nicole Benedict. I don't have an appointment." And it was a good bet Ethan wouldn't recognize her name.

Heck, she'd be surprised if he recognized her face. It had only been a couple of months since they'd met at Hitchin' My Getalong, a hokey themed bar in the heart of the city, but the handsome, brooding stranger hadn't been real sober when she'd hitched her getalong up onto the bar stool beside him.

Okay, *neither* of them had been real sober that night.

"Sign in here." The guard handed over a digital pad that reminded Nicole of the ones the courier guy used when he delivered her research supplies.

The thought brought a wince. Unless she found a new sponsor for her biofuel project at Donner High School, the research would be doomed before the school year started. Then again, ten weeks ago, the conjunction of the defunct sponsorship, her thirty-fourth birthday and the one-year anniversary of her ex-engagement to Jonah I-prefer-blondes Douglas had been the most important things in her universe.

How quickly things change, she thought as she used the plastic wand to scrawl her name, destination and the time she'd entered the building onto the pressure pad. She glanced at the blank "time out" box and tried not to wonder how long her meeting would take. What Ethan would say.

Swallowing hard, she accepted a visitor's badge from the guard and headed for the elevator. The deep blue carpet was springy underfoot. The elevator doors were made of copper-colored metal, and etched with repeating symbols that reminded her of the Navajo blanket on her bed. A classy plaque beside the call buttons bore the names of the megadollar companies that leased space in the downtown skyscraper. Prescott Personal Securities was listed at the very bottom, indicating that it was located on the top floor. Prime real estate.

Way out of your league, Nicky girl. You're suburbs. This is city. The thought came in Jonah's voice, complete with her ex-fiancé's trademark smirk, which she'd found charming for entirely too long.

"Oh, shut up," she said, and stabbed the elevator call button.

Moments later, the etched copper doors parted to reveal an aquarium. Okay, so technically it was a glass-enclosed elevator car, but Nic felt distinctly guppyish as she stepped inside and several street-level passersby glanced in her direction.

"Keep it moving, nothing to see here," she

muttered as she hit the button for the top floor. "Just a pregnant woman in a see-through box."

She wasn't showing at ten weeks, of course, but ever since the doctor had confirmed what four at-home tests had already told her, she'd felt as though she had the words *unmarried and knocked-up by a one-night stand* tattooed across her forehead.

The elevator doors hissed shut and the car ascended with expensive smoothness. The glass floor pressed against the soles of her sneakers, seeming hard and impersonal after the give of the lobby carpet. Unease flickered when she realized there were no supporting metal braces beneath her feet. Just more glass.

"It's perfectly safe," she told herself, scrubbing her damp palms against her jeans and tugging at her pale yellow sweater set. "Don't be a wuss."

Besides, she was pretty sure the nerves had nothing to do with the elevator and everything to do with her errand. What would she say when she saw Ethan again? More importantly, what would *he* say?

Nic swallowed hard and forced herself to focus on the view.

The Denver streets stretched out below, gleaming in the noonday sun. Buildings rose on either side of her, then fell away as the elevator carried her above the neighboring structures. The blue sky stretched to the edge of the city bowl miles away, where the Rocky Mountains spread across the horizon. A few clouds scudded high above, and the translucent glass paneling of the elevator made it seem as though she could stretch out and touch the fluffy white vapor.

When movement flickered in her peripheral vision, she turned, expecting a bird. Instead, she saw a snub-nosed helicopter.

Her first thought was that it had to be a traffic 'copter, but the shiny black machine didn't bear the call letters of any local station. In fact, the chopper was completely unmarked, with dull black patches where its FAA identification should have been.

Nic's heart picked up when the chopper drew nearer and the thump of rotors vibrated through the glass. She craned her neck to see if a second helicopter was filming whatever was going on. A reality show, maybe, or an action movie.

There was no sign of a camera crew as the

unmarked helicopter swung around to face her, broadside.

Nic saw a pilot and two passengers, their features blurred by motion and distance. As she watched, a door rolled open and a large, muscular figure climbed out to perch on one skid. He hefted something onto his shoulder. It looked a whole lot like a rocket launcher.

Still no sign of a film crew.

Panic spurted and a scream built in Nic's throat. Disbelieving, she stumbled to the back of the elevator; her spine slammed into the control panel, and the car jolted to a shuddering halt. An alarm bell shrilled, the sound muted by her scream as the man aimed the launcher directly at her.

A disembodied voice spoke from an intercom panel above her head. "This is building security. Is everything okay in there?"

Nic shrieked, "There's a helicopter outside, and a man and he's going to—"

Everything exploded.

ONE MINUTE Ethan Moore was in his little-used cube at Prescott Personal Securities, cursing his computer. The next moment, noise blasted around him like a thousand Humvees converging on a single spot, and he was sent flying through the air.

Shouting in surprise, Ethan rolled when he hit, trying to get away from pelting debris, but it was everywhere. Old training and newer instincts kicked in, laced with adrenaline as the floor shuddered beneath him and metal groaned.

A bomb, he thought, though experience told him that wasn't quite right.

He scrambled to his hands and knees, head ringing. The too-hot fabric of his cargo pants and button-down shirt scorched against his skin. Acrid smoke stung his nose, eyes and throat, and he felt himself coughing but couldn't hear the noise over the ringing in his ears.

A second explosion ripped through the office. He ducked and shouted with rage. Disbelief. How had the bomber gotten through their security? How had—

Never mind, he told himself. *Logic, not emotion. Evacuate first, then figure out who's behind the attack.* Though there was no doubt in his mind Tri Corp. Media was behind the attack. Over the past five months,

PPS had been struggling to uncover who was behind a vicious string of murderous attacks on their protectees. Now that they were hot on the trail of several higher-ups at the huge media conglomerate, the faceless mastermind had only sped things up.

Gasping smoke-laced oxygen, Ethan dragged himself to his feet as the noise of the explosion subsided. The smoke and fire alarms cut in, shrilling over the screams and curses that rose up from the other cubes.

"Everyone stay calm!" Ethan shouted in a voice he barely recognized as his own. He looked quickly around the high-tech office space, counting heads. Twelve men and women, all support staff. Most of the other PPS field agents were out chasing leads. Meanwhile, TCM had brought the fight home.

"You!" Ethan pointed to the closest sturdy-looking guy, a computer tech with a nasty gash below one eye. "Check all the cubes. If the wounded are ambulatory, get them out. If not, come find me. And for God's sake, don't move anyone who's down and injured."

Next, Ethan located their receptionist, Angel, a twenty-something woman wearing black clothes, black lipstick and a diamond stud in her nose. Knowing her penchant for fouling up even the simplest tasks, he kept it simple. "Pop the security doors so everyone can get out. Use the stairs, not the elevators. Got it?"

The terrified-looking receptionist swallowed hard. "Where are you going?"

"To find the boss," Ethan said, and headed farther into the office suite without looking back.

He wasn't leaving without Evangeline Prescott.

A few weeks earlier, her name had turned up on a list that included the half-dozen men who'd been murdered over the past few months as part of a deadly billion-dollar oil rights conspiracy. Evangeline was no investor, but the list suggested she was a target.

And the blast had come from the direction of her corner office.

Cursing, Ethan skirted the cube farm, dodging the debris and fluttering papers that swirled on the wind whipping through broken windows. The temperature rose as he headed toward the corner suite, heat crackling on his skin.

"Evangeline, are you in there?" he shouted. "Robert? You okay?"

Ethan called Evangeline's husband's name as an afterthought. He didn't know PPS's original founder well, and what he knew didn't impress him much. Robert Prescott had reappeared the previous month after having spent the past two years underground, trying to figure out who'd set him up to die in a rigged plane crash that now appeared to have been one of the earliest moves in the TCM conspiracy, orchestrated by Robert's former mentor in the world of international espionage. The way Ethan saw it, whether he was a real-life James Bond or not, a man shouldn't ever let anything except actual death separate him from the woman he'd loved.

Life-and-death danger had a way of leveling differences though, so when Ethan stuck his head through the doorway leading to Robert's office and called the man's name, he felt a sharp twist of relief when he got an answer.

"Over here," Robert said, voice cracking. The room was in shambles, with the desk overturned and wedged against one wall. The founder of PPS was trapped beneath the desk with only his salt-and-pepper hair and one blood-smeared hand visible. The hand waved and Robert's voice carried the hint of a British accent and the authority of his MI6 background when he ordered, "Get this bloody thing off me."

Emotion wanted to send Ethan bolting across the room to help his fallen comrade. Logic had him pausing to test the floor, which was tipped at an angle beneath his feet. When it seemed sturdy enough, he crossed the room, looked at how Robert was pinned, and levered a corner of the desk up and away.

After a quick field check for major injuries, Ethan hauled Robert to his feet. "Angel's got the blast doors open. Take the stairs."

Robert swiped a hand across a bloody gash on his cheek. "Bugger that. Where's my wife?"

Though Robert and Evangeline's relationship had been bumpy since he'd returned from the dead, Ethan heard the raw grief in the other man's voice. Trying not to resent Robert's right to that grief, Ethan turned away. "Let's go find her."

The men ducked out of Robert's office, crossed the short distance to Evangeline's door and stopped dead.

A low groan rattled in Robert's chest.

Beyond the door, dust and smoke blurred the sight of the mountains in the distance. There was no outer wall. Hell, there was no office. It had become a crater in the side of the building. Heat radiated from the remnants of walls, floor and ceiling. Black soot smeared the carpeting beneath their feet, and the floor beyond fell away to air.

Robert sagged against the door frame.

"God," Ethan rasped. "I'm so—"

"Don't say it," Robert snapped. "Don't even think it. She's not dead. She can't be dead, not when we've just found each other again."

You knew where she was all along, you selfish bastard. An angry ball congealed in Ethan's gut, alongside the grief. *You have no idea what it was like for her, what it feels like to lose someone you love.*

But because Ethan *did* know, he said, "Let's check the other offices, and the break rooms. The bathroom. Maybe—" He broke off when he heard a faint sound.

Robert heard it, too. He spun and bolted down the hall, shouting, "Evangeline? Evangeline, damn it, answer me!" He skidded to a halt outside the small kitchenette they used as a break room. "She's in here!"

Then he cursed viciously enough to jab fear into Ethan's gut.

When he reached the doorway, Ethan saw that the floor tilted away from them and down, as though all the support beams were gone. The refrigerator had tipped over, spilling its contents onto the floor. The chairs and tables were all lodged against the far wall, with Evangeline trapped beneath them.

The tall, forty-something blonde was bleeding but conscious. She and Robert locked eyes and she smiled with relief. "You're okay."

He made an unintelligible sound, and when he reached out a hand as though he could touch her across the distance separating them, his fingers trembled.

Dark emotion rose up to clog Ethan's throat, a blend of relief, resentment and hell, yes, jealousy. Not because he wanted Evangeline, but because he hadn't gotten a second chance with the woman he'd loved, and Prescott seemed to get nothing but second chances.

"I'll get her," Robert said. "You check the rest of the offices." Ethan nodded shortly and turned away, but before he'd gone more than a few steps, Prescott called, "Did your client get out okay?"

Ethan stopped and looked back. "I'm not scheduled to see anyone today."

"Angel left a message a few minutes ago on my voice mail," Robert said. "She said a client was on her way up to see you."

Ethan didn't bother asking why she'd left the info with Robert—Angel lost half their messages and garbled the other half, but she was one of Evangeline's projects, so firing her wasn't an option.

"I haven't met with anyone all morning," he said now, a faint alarm stirring in the back of his skull. "Did you get a name?"

"I think she said Nicole Benedict. Ring any bells?"

The faint alarm became a war whoop as the name did more than ring a bell. It sent a lightning bolt through Ethan's midsection, a mixture of guilt, regret and pure, unadulterated lust.

Air hissed between his teeth at the thought of the woman who'd helped him forget himself for a night, then disappeared. "Yeah. I know her. And if she was on the way up—" He broke off on a second hiss of breath as logic overtook emotion and he remembered that the track for the glass elevator ran along the outside of the building, right beside Evangeline's office. It would've been right in the path of the explosion.

He took off at a dead run, hoping to hell he wasn't already too late.

NICOLE REGAINED fuzzy consciousness to the feel of something cold and hard beneath her face. For half a second, she wondered what the hell she was doing lying on her kitchen floor. And why were her ears ringing? Was she hungover?

But that wasn't right. She'd never been much of a partyer, and wasn't drinking at all these days because of—

The connection sparked in her brain and clenched her stomach in an instant. *The baby. Ethan. Prescott Personal Securities.* Images blinked through her mind in rapid succession—the office building, the helicopter, the rocket launcher—

The explosion.

Her eyes flew open and she found herself face-down on the floor of the glassed-in elevator. She saw the street far below. Then a thin stream of blackish-gray smoke obscured her view for a moment, and the contrast showed her something far worse than the height. There was a crack in the glass beneath her.

As she watched, it grew longer and branched into two cracks that gave birth to two more in a growing spiderweb that weakened the only thing separating her from a fatal fall.

"Help me," she whispered, half-afraid the small sound might send her crashing through. When it didn't, she filled her lungs and screamed, *"Help me!"*

Incredibly, a man's voice answered from above. "Hang on, Nicole. I'm almost there."

"Ethan?" She wasn't sure how she recognized his voice, ten weeks after they'd spent the night together doing everything but talking, but she knew him instantly, and the recognition brought a fierce rush of relief edged with fear.

"Don't move." His words sounded clearer than they ought to, and she heard the whistle of wind.

Fearing what she might see, Nic held her breath and tried to keep her body still as she turned her head to the side. She saw more glass, more cracks, and a gaping hole in the side of the elevator car, where the glass was gone. Beyond that was blue sky, a smudge of smoke and a dangling climber's rope. She heard masculine shouts from higher up, a mixture of suggestions and curses from whoever was anchoring the line.

She remembered him saying something about rock climbing in his free time. Now he was shimmying down to rescue her. God.

As she watched, a pair of sturdy, brown leather hiking boots swung into her limited slice of view, followed by a hint of tube sock and a pair of strong, muscular legs encased in tough-looking cargo pants and a make-shift climber's harness. The button-down front of a formerly white oxford shirt appeared next, gaping where a couple of buttons had torn away to reveal a lean, muscular torso.

Then he twisted through the broken section of glass, and she got a clear look at the edgy, masculine face she'd imagined all too often since realizing her period was late.

Hell, she thought, *let's be honest here. You've thought about him just about every day since that night at Hitchin's.* And she'd remembered him just right. His dark brown hair was lighter at the ends, signaling an outdoor lifestyle. His face was chiseled, his features as sharp and forbidding as she'd remembered. Now, though, the brown eyes she remembered as being coolly logical and almost sardonic, radiated tension as they locked on hers and he said, "Stay calm. We can do this, but you've got to trust me, okay?" He waited until she nodded, then said, "I want you to keep yourself flat and distribute your weight as evenly as possible. Then I need you to slide toward me. We're going to get you out of there."

Nic's breath hissed out. She glanced down and saw emergency vehicles gathering far below. "I can't… I won't…" She stopped and sucked in a breath. "Can't you open the doors from inside the building?"

"Not a chance. You're—" He broke off, looked up as the rescue personnel shouted something she didn't quite catch, and muttered a curse. "Look, the explosion knocked the elevator off its track, okay? It's hanging by a single cable right now. It looks stable enough, but—"

A loud crackling noise cut him off, and the floor shifted beneath Nic. She whimpered deep in her throat and tears stung her eyes. "Ethan, please," she whispered. "The floor's going to go. I don't want to die."

"Slide over," he repeated, speaking softly. "Go easy, but keep moving, no matter what happens."

Heart pounding in her ears, Nic closed her eyes, pressed her cheek to the floor and slid an inch, then another. She heard crackling, but didn't look at the glass beneath her.

"That's it. You're almost there."

He sounded closer, prompting Nic to open her eyes. He'd dropped lower on the rope, so their faces were level through the broken panel.

His voice might be utterly calm, but his eyes held a strange, dark emotion she couldn't quite define.

An answering surge tugged in her chest, the same feeling she'd had when she'd offered to buy him a drink and he'd turned to refuse, then accepted instead. Now, though, there was an added layer between them, the echoing heat of sex…and a baby he'd never know about if she fell.

"Ethan," Nic whispered, heart pounding. "I came to tell you I'm pregnant."

She might've imagined the wince, but there was no mistaking his low curse, or the look that flashed through his eyes before he shuttered his expression to one of utter determination and stretched his arm through the broken side of the elevator car. "We need to get you on solid ground. Take my hand."

She looked from him to the ground and back again. When her weight shifted, the glass beneath her cracked further.

"Come on." His eyes were steady on hers, his outstretched hand unwavering. "Trust me."

Heart pounding loud in her ears, she reached out and grabbed his forearm, just as the crackling noise crescendoed—

And the glass gave way beneath her.

Nic screamed as she fell and then jerked to a suspended halt, dangling in Ethan's grip, held only by their joined hands. Sobbing, terrified, she grabbed for him with her free hand as a roaring, crumbling noise built overhead, counterpointed by pinging metal.

She looked up and shrieked, "Ethan! The cable!"

Overhead, the elevator mechanism was coming apart.

He twisted his head and shouted to the men leaning out of a window two floors up. "Pull us in, damn it!" His expression remained impassive, but his voice was sharp when he said, "You're going to have to climb up through the hole in the elevator floor before it goes. Watch the broken glass."

The next two minutes were a blur as Nic scrambled, fighting for purchase as he pulled her up and out, helped by the uniformed rescue personnel two floors up, who were cursing and hauling on the rope as fast as they dared.

Then she was out! She lunged through the open panel and launched herself against Ethan just as the elevator gave way with a horrendous crack and plummeted down, trailing broken cables. Momentum sent them spinning, and Nic hung on tightly as they swung away from the building. She felt Ethan's strong body against hers, felt his heart drum fast through the fabric of his shirt. Then the arc reversed and they went flying back toward the building.

"Hang on!" Ethan swung them so he'd bear the brunt, but an errant wind gust caught them and diverted the spin, changing their angle of impact.

Nic hit first, and she hit hard. The blow drove the breath from her lungs. Her neck whiplashed and her head slammed into the side of the building.

Starbursts flashed in her head, and then every sensation was abruptly sucked into a black void. Every sensation, that is, except the feel of the man who held her tight.

Chapter Two

Ethan's muscles worked automatically, stabilizing them against the side of the building and cradling Nicole's unconscious body as the rescue personnel hauled them up, but his brain was jammed full. One part of him cataloged her injuries—she'd taken a hell of a whack to the head—while another, deeper part of him processed her announcement.

The last thing he'd expected—or wanted—to hear was that she was pregnant.

Then again, he'd never actually figured he'd see her again. The morning after their night together, he'd filed the memory in the tiny Pleasant Interludes section of his brain and walked away. Maybe he'd thought of her once or twice in the months since. And maybe he'd stuck his head into Hitchin's a couple of times since. But a baby? God, no.

They'd been careful. He'd used a condom, damn it.

But there was that whole ninety-nine-point-nine-percent-effective thing. Apparently, he'd stepped straight into that point-oh-one of *oh, hell.*

"We've got her," a male voice said, breaking into Ethan's thoughts. He was startled to realize they'd reached the place where a bank of broken windows had allowed him to climb down to the elevator. The rescue personnel almost hadn't let him go, but he was the one with the rock-climbing equipment and the skills, and there hadn't been time to wait for the real search-and-rescue team.

It was just dumb luck he'd had his gear in the office, dumb luck that'd he'd been able to save Nicole's life.

Suited firefighters leaned through, reaching to grab her unconscious form and ease her to relative safety indoors.

"Careful," Ethan said unnecessarily. "She's—" *Pregnant,* he thought, but couldn't say the word. "She banged her head pretty hard."

It'd happened so fast he hadn't been able

to protect her from slamming into the building. She was breathing fine, but she was still unconscious. What had it been, two minutes? Five? *Too long.*

Jaw set, he climbed through, shucked off his harness and stowed his gear, then jogged to catch up with the group of paramedics who were carrying Nicole down the stairs, strapped to a backboard.

As the small group emerged into the early-afternoon sunlight, one of the paramedics glanced up at the smoke that continued to pour from the ruined PPS offices. "Looks like the building will hold, thank the Lord."

There was a murmur of agreement from the others, but Ethan didn't join in. Instead, he scanned the street, which was a scene of barely controlled chaos. Most of the evacuees and onlookers had been pushed back, away from the damaged office building, but dazed-looking people continued to stream from the stairwells. Nearby, several wickedly jagged cement chunks were embedded in a cracked section of sidewalk, surrounded by the glitter of reflective glass shards. Off to one side, a scattering of first aid supplies ringed a dark stain.

The explosion had taken victims outside the building as well as in, Ethan thought, feeling the acid burn of anger in his gut.

"Ethan!"

He turned at the sound of Robert's voice, and saw PPS's founder loping across the deserted street toward him. The men gripped each other's fore-arms in greeting, the first friendly contact Ethan could remember between them. "How's Evangeline?" he asked.

"She'll need a few stitches, but is fine otherwise. She's spitting mad. Wants to take a chunk out of the bomber." The last was said with a touch of pride.

"I'll ditto that." Half his attention on the paramedics, who were busy transferring Nicole to a gurney, Ethan gestured to the stained sidewalk. "Pedestrian?"

Robert nodded, expression darkening. "Falling debris caught a mother and her two kids. Doesn't look good for the little girl."

"Damn." Ethan scowled. It had been bad enough when the mastermind had started killing off TCM's investors one by one. It had been worse when they'd murdered a PPS computer tech and then slapped Evangeline's name on the list, but at the very least those targets had been logical. Now they'd escalated way beyond that to injuring innocent bystanders… like the mother and her children. Like Nicole, who'd come to tell him he was a father.

Ethan glanced over at her, seeing the beauty beneath the oxygen mask as the paramedics loaded her into the waiting ambulance.

Her face had popped into his head more often than he cared to admit in the weeks since he'd met her.

That night, a friend's wedding—and the memories it'd brought—had chased him out of the reception and into a tourist-trap bar. He hadn't noticed her at first, hadn't had eyes for much other than the glass in front of him. He would've had to have been dead, though, to miss noticing when she leaned across him to snag a napkin, pressing against him just long enough to let him know she was looking to play.

He'd been struck first by her dark curls, then by her eyes, which were a strangely intense shade of blue, bordering on violet. Rimmed by dark lashes, they'd looked moments away from laughter all the time, even when she'd been serious. During those serious moments, she'd caught her full lower lip between her teeth, an action that'd left him hard and wanting.

Then later, once the small talk was done and they were alone in the hotel room they'd rented because neither of them had been sober enough to drive home, she'd caught her bottom lip in her teeth again at the moment of her climax, prompting him to capture that lower lip with his own mouth and nibble it into submission.

Afterward, she'd looked at him with a hint of wonder in those violet eyes, a hint of shyness. All an act, he'd thought at first, designed to keep a bar conquest intrigued. But during the long hours of the night, small inconsistencies had added up in his carefully logical brain, leaving him wondering whether that night had been as out of character for her as it had been for him.

He'd resigned himself to never knowing for sure. Now, it seemed he'd been given a second chance to find out.

"Did you hear me?" Robert said, tone sharp.

"Sorry," Ethan said without looking at his

boss. "How about I meet you and Evangeline at the hospital?"

"You need a ride?"

"I'm all set." He strode toward the ambulance they'd loaded Nicole into, only to stop and turn back when Robert called his name. "What?" he said, voice edgy with impatience and something more, something he didn't want to analyze too closely.

Robert looked from Ethan to the ambulance and back. "Who is she?"

"She's—" Ethan broke off, not sure what she was. She wasn't a friend, wasn't his lover, yet she'd come to tell him she was carrying his child. "She's not a client," he said shortly, and headed for the ambulance.

They'd figure out the rest once she woke up.

TERRIFIED, Nicole screamed and batted at the blurry shadows around her, fighting the feeling of weightlessness, of falling.

Then she was on the ground without hitting bottom, and something was pressing her down, trapping her arms and legs. She screamed again and fought the hold. "Let me go!"

A man's voice said, "Nicole, you're okay. You're safe. Calm down and listen to me. You're in the hospital, not the elevator. You're okay." The words were more rough than soothing, but they calmed her while sending up a strange shimmy inside.

She woke further, feeling warmth where his hands gripped her forearms. The voice and touch were familiar, but she couldn't think of his name, couldn't picture his face, and that brought a spurt of renewed panic, which took up residence alongside a pounding headache.

Opening her eyes, she squinted into the night-dim lights of a hospital room and saw a tall man wearing wrinkled khaki bush pants and a smudged white button-down missing a couple of buttons. His dark brown hair brushed over his forehead, streaked with highlights she imagined might be gold in better light. His eyes were dark brown and intelligent beneath heavy brows, his nose aquiline, his jaw chiseled. The whole effect was compelling and more than a little distant.

And it was a stranger's face.

"Why am I in the hospital?" she demanded. "Who are you?"

Before he could answer, the hallway door swung open and a white-coated, dark-haired female doctor entered. Her expression softened when she looked at the bed. "It's good to see you awake, Miss Benedict."

Panic pounded through Nic as she pointed to the man. "I don't know him."

The doctor pursed her lips, leaned down and flashed a penlight in Nic's eyes. "Follow this." She kept up a background monologue as she ran through a quick exam. "I'm Dr. Eballa—that's with an *a* and two *l*'s, please, not Ebola like the virus." She paused and wrote something on a clipboard, then said, "Your vitals are good and everything checks out normal, but you've got a good-sized knot on the back of your head and you were out for quite a while." She straightened away from the bed. "What's your full name and what are your parents' names?"

"Nicole Antoinette Benedict," Nic said immediately. "My parents are Lyle and Mary Benedict. They live back in Maryland where I grew up." The easy answers calmed some of the panic and she shifted and lifted a hand to the back of her head, wincing when she found a tender, raised bump the size of her palm. "What happened?"

"What is the last thing you remember?"

"I—" Nicole broke off, her stomach twisting when she realized that while she remembered lots of things, they weren't in any sort of order. She could picture a greenhouse full of plants, but she wasn't sure if it was a memory from last week or last year. Panic spiked through the pounding headache, and her voice trembled when she said, "I don't know."

The doctor touched her wrist, maybe in reassurance, maybe a quick check on her pulse. "That's not uncommon after a concussion such as yours. Things should start to clear up over the next few hours or days, though you may never remember the actual attack."

Nic's blood iced in her veins. "I was *attacked?*"

"Not you personally," the man said. "You were in an elevator when the building was bombed."

"Bombed!" Something shivered just out of Nic's mental reach, a flash of sunlight on a dark shape, there and then gone so quickly she wasn't sure it had ever been. She closed

her eyes for a second, scared and frustrated at the same time. "I don't remember." She glanced at him. "And I'm sorry, I don't know your name. Are we…" She trailed off, not sure what she meant to ask.

As she fumbled, Dr. Eballa stepped away from the bed and adjusted the lights higher. The man turned and scowled in the doctor's direction.

Instantly, his image was overlain by another in her mind's eye. It was the same face but a different setting—a bar, crowded, noisy and dark. He'd turned and scowled at her, but his brown eyes had warmed with reluctant interest when she'd said something clever—she didn't remember what it had been, but no matter. She remembered him stretching out a hand, remembered the warmth and the faint electric buzz when they shook and he'd said, "I'm—"

"Ethan!" she said aloud in the hospital room, making him jump.

A flash of relief glinted in his eyes, tainted with something more complicated. "You remember."

"I remember meeting you in a bar, and…" She trailed off as other memories reconnected. The bar hookup. The hotel room. Hot sex. A plus sign on the home pregnancy test when she'd been praying for a minus. "Oh," she said, then more forcefully, "*Oh!* Oh, no. I have to talk to you. In private."

He turned away, as though he didn't want her to read his eyes when he said, "You already told me about the baby."

"Oh." She swallowed hard and tried to fight through the headache and a growing swell of nausea. "I don't remember that." *What did I say?* she wanted to ask. *What did you say?*

"What is the last thing you *do* remember?" he demanded, and she had a feeling there was more to the question than him judging the extent of her partial amnesia.

"I remember getting up this morning." She glanced at him. "Is it Tuesday?" When he nodded, she felt a small measure of relief. "Then I remember getting up this morning. I read the paper and made a few calls for a project I'm working on." Pitifully unsuccessful calls, she remembered. "Then I drove into the city to see you. I can picture myself parking somewhere and walking into a big building, but I'm not sure if that's a memory or a logical guess."

"You don't remember being in a glass-walled elevator?" he persisted.

She shook her head, then winced and pressed her fingers to her temples when the headache spiked.

"You're hurting." He stepped away from the bed. "I'll come back later."

"No." The terror had subsided somewhat with the piecemeal return of her memory. In its place was a sense of urgency. Despite what had happened at the office building, she'd set out that morning with a purpose. Now, she looked at Dr. Eballa and saw compassion in the other woman's eyes. "Can we have a few minutes alone?"

The doctor hesitated a beat, then nodded. "You're lucid, and it's not unexpected for you to have blocked out the actual trauma. You may never remember that chunk of time, but everything else seems okay. I'll take a walk. When you and Mr. Moore are finished, I'll come back and run a few more tests, just to be on the safe side."

When she was gone, Nic stared at her legs beneath the pale blue hospital blanket. "In case you were wondering, there's no chance the baby could be any-one else's."

He nodded, though she didn't know if that meant he believed her, or if that was what he'd expected her to say. Which just underscored how much she didn't know about the father of her unborn child. She'd picked him up in a bar, for heaven's sake, and though she'd like to think she wouldn't have been attracted to a jerk, her track record said otherwise.

"Do you…" She faltered, but pushed through the awkwardness with a faint thread of optimism. "What do you think about being a father?"

"Being a sperm donor doesn't make a man a father," he said, voice nearly inflectionless, but he paced the length of the room, body language giving voice to the upset within.

When he stopped at the window and worked the mechanism to open the blinds and look out at the night, she thought she saw something sad in the reflection of his eyes, something that defused her quick anger and left the hurt behind.

"I'm sorry," he said after a moment. "It's not about you, or about what we did. It's…"

He turned toward her and spread his hands away from his long, lean body. "Let's just say the world is better off if I'm in it by myself."

A flare of disappointment warned Nic that no matter how many times she'd told herself not to think foolish thoughts, some piece of her had been hoping for the happy nuclear family she'd always dreamed of. But she forced her voice level when she said, "I didn't come looking for a marriage proposal. Lucky for us, society has evolved past shotgun weddings."

Though she had a feeling her professor father's reaction wouldn't be particularly evolved when he found out his first—and possibly only—grandchild would be born outside of wedlock.

Ethan repeated, "I'm sorry."

"Me, too," she said. "I wish…" She trailed off, not sure what exactly she wished. If she hadn't gone into Hitchin's that night, damned caution and hiked up onto a bar stool beside the hottest guy in the joint, she would've missed out on some pretty fabulous sex. And yes, she would've missed out on the life growing inside her. An unplanned life, perhaps, but one she already cherished.

"I'm okay with it, really," she said, not sure whether she was saying it for his benefit or her own. "I've always planned on having kids. Even thought I'd found the right guy once."

"Jonah," he said, surprising her.

She nodded, remembering that she'd mentioned her ex in passing during their brief bar flirtation. "Good memory. But that—obviously—didn't work out."

Ethan looked over his shoulder at her. "Was that why you were at Hitchin's that night? Because of him?"

"No," she said quickly, then stopped herself and went with the truth. "Or, not really. It was my thirty-fourth birthday that day. I had all these plans with my friends from the school." She glanced at him. "Did I tell you I'm a teacher?" When he shook his head, she said, "Science. Donner High School. Anyway, we were supposed to have a girls' day out—a few hours at the spa, a movie, that sort of thing. Simple fun. But I got up that morning, looked in the mirror, and all I saw was someone I never expected to be. Thirty-four, unmarried, no kids."

She shook her head. "That much I

could've dealt with. I'd been dealing just fine. But then I checked my messages and found out that Toulouse Inc. was backing out of funding this biofuel project I've been working on with some of my students. We've built this great greenhouse." She sketched the building with her hands. "Corn. Wheat. Soybeans. Easily renewable resources. And we've got a converter we designed..." She trailed off, aware that he was staring. "And I'm babbling. You don't care about any of this. Sorry."

Jonah had always hated when she'd interjected her "little project" into dinner-party conversation, even though it had been his idea that she leave grad school for the more family-friendly schedule of teaching high school. The way she figured it, if Jonah hadn't cared about the biofuel project, then Ethan certainly wouldn't.

"Sorry," she said again when he just stared at her. She felt a hot flush climb her cheeks. "That's not what you're here to talk about, is it? You want to settle things, make sure I'm okay. Well, I am." She took a deep breath to quell the taint of nausea at the back of her throat. "I didn't go looking for you because

I wanted a proposal, or money or anything like that. I'm fully prepared to have this baby and raise it on my own. Heck, I'm looking forward to it. If I'm lucky, I'll meet a man and fall in love with him, and the three of us can make a family, make more babies, have the white picket fence, the Labrador and the whole nine yards." She paused, then continued, "But that doesn't change the fact that this baby is half yours, so I needed to tell you about him or her. What you do with the information is pretty much up to you."

She was babbling again, she realized. Or maybe she was speaking normally and it just felt like babbling because Ethan was so reserved, so remote.

Still standing by the window, silhouetted against the darkness, he inclined his head in a brief nod. "Thanks for telling me. And I'm sorry you got caught up in what happened back at PPS. I just need… I need to take a walk." He glanced from her to the door and back. "Don't go anywhere until I get back."

"Where am I going to go?" she said, but he was already gone, the door swinging shut at his back, leaving her alone in silence broken by the faint hum of fluorescent lights and ventilation, the sense of movement and activity just beyond the door.

Nic sat for a second, not sure how she felt other than sore everywhere, and unbelievably tired.

Well, that was over. She wasn't sure if she was more relieved or disappointed. She felt hollow, drained of just about everything. Her headache had even subsided, leaving her vaguely restless.

She glanced down, making sure she wasn't hooked to any machines before she sat up in the hospital bed. When that earned her only a long, lazy spin of the room and a thump of the headache, she decided to try using the bathroom. If she could make it there and back under her own steam, she was doing okay. Maybe even okay enough to go home.

Suddenly, she couldn't think of anything more appealing than her four-room apartment with the soft Navajo blanket on the bed.

"Bathroom first," she said aloud. Suiting action to word, she threw back the blankets and swung her legs over the side of the bed. Her feet were numb and her whole body felt disconnected, as though her head was floating along under its own power as she made it across the room, nearly to the bathroom door.

Out of the corner of her eyes, she saw a dark shadow through the window of the hallway door. The shadow paused, then pushed through.

Nic turned, expecting a lecture from Dr. Eballa. "I was just—" She broke off because it wasn't her doctor. It was an unshaven, heavyset man wearing a white lab coat over a T-shirt, jeans and heavy boots.

He grabbed her before she could react, and covered her mouth with his hand.

Panic spurted as Nic screamed against his palm. She struggled, kicking him with her bare feet and scratching at him with her fingernails. He didn't react, just held on as she felt a prick in her upper arm, then a fiery sizzle in her veins that quickly faded to cool numbness.

Aware of her surroundings but unable to stay upright, she slumped to the floor and hit hard. He pushed through the door for a moment, then returned, pulling a gurney behind him. He grabbed her around the waist, heaved her up onto the gurney and covered her most of the way with the blanket from her bed.

Then he wheeled her out of the room.

Chapter Three

Ethan walked the hospital corridors with no real destination in mind. He simply thought better when he was moving. He always had.

Nicole's child might have half his DNA, but he knew as well as anyone that biology didn't make a father. Character made a man a father. Honesty did, and integrity. Wholeness.

And though Ethan considered himself a logical, honest man, he was anything but whole.

Seeing a knot of people in the hallway up ahead, he detoured down the next offshoot corridor. If he'd still believed in the religion his mother had tried to instill in him, he might've thought it no accident that the hallway dead-ended at the hospital chapel. Since he'd long ago renounced faith in a higher power, he thought only that it was a quiet, empty space with padded benches.

He sprawled in one, let his head fall back with a thump and closed his eyes.

Just that morning, everything had been normal. True, the TCM investigation was way beyond PPS's usual cases, but that was work, not personal. Over the past five years he'd done his best to insulate himself against letting things get personal. If he wasn't involved, he couldn't be hurt.

More importantly, he couldn't hurt anyone else.

"Ethan?" Evangeline's voice said from nearby. "Is everything okay?"

Though he normally enjoyed her company, his first thought now was *oh, hell.*

He cracked his lids and watched her sit in the pew across the aisle from him. She was wearing the top half of a set of scrubs, along with her own pants and shoes. Her right arm was bandaged from shoulder to elbow, and a Band-Aid above her left eyebrow was several shades darker than her pale skin. But she looked steady enough as she said, "What's wrong?"

"Where's Robert?"

"Why, because you and he are both Neanderthal enough to think it's his job to keep me under control?" She sent him her trademark give-me-a-break look. "For your information I've been treated and released. No hospital room, no observation period. I'm fit and ready to get back into the fight." She flexed her good arm, showing a decent muscle, but he noticed that she didn't try it with the bandaged arm. "And to answer your other question, Robert is on the phone with one of his police contacts, trying to get an update on what the crime scene analysts and the bomb squad think about the office."

"Still, you shouldn't be walking around alone," Ethan said.

She sent him a sharp look. "I ran PPS by myself for more than two years, during which time, I might add, I hired you. Just because Robert rose from the dead doesn't make me incapable of defending myself."

He shook his head. "I didn't say you were, but your name is on the hit list and your office took the brunt of the attack. You have to be careful. We can't afford to lose you."

If Robert had begun to reemerge as the leader of PPS, Evangeline was the glue that held them together. She had drawn Ethan into the organization, giving him the base of support he'd so badly needed, along with the freedom to take short-term protection assignments that suited his short-term attention span.

"I can take care of myself," Evangeline repeated. "I'm not going to do anything stupid, though. And don't think I didn't notice you changing the subject. So give. Why're you sitting in here alone?"

"I like being alone." But the question brought his mind circling back to Nicole.

She was going to have a baby. His baby.

What the hell was he supposed to do about that? Nothing, he knew. It would be better for everyone involved if he did nothing. His own father had been a sperm donor, his stepfather a savior. Nicole and the baby would be far better off finding a man to complete their family without living the hell his own mother had suffered through to find her Prince Charming.

Besides, a family meant commitment and emotion, neither of which were rational choices for someone like him.

Evangeline waited for him to continue. When he didn't, she said, "It's an open-ended offer with no statue of limitations. So if you need a friend to talk to, come find me, okay?"

Ethan dipped his chin in a nod. "Thanks."

She stood, mostly covering her wince. "Robert and I are headed over to the Vault." Her eyes glinted with determination, along with rising anger. "PPS will be run from there until this thing is finished."

"The Vault?" Intrigued despite himself, Ethan climbed to his feet and followed her out of the chapel. "I thought that was an in-house urban legend." Rumor had it that PPS maintained a secret underground location, and had spy ware in place to duplicate every piece of information that came and went from the PPS offices, sending it to the Vault.

"It's real," Evangeline said with a small smile. "It's located in an old Cold War bunker outside the city. With the main office destroyed, we're going to move operations there. A couple of the guys are organizing the support staff, figuring out who we absolutely can't do without, and getting them set up underground." Her lips thinned. "It's coming down to the wire, Ethan. Either we take out whoever is behind that list or they take us out."

She pushed through the door leading to the hallway, with Ethan right behind her. Just then, heavy footsteps rang out around the corner, the sound of a big man, moving fast.

Ethan stepped in front of Evangeline, tensing for battle, then relaxing when Robert appeared.

The other man's expression was tight. "Is Miss Benedict with you two?"

"She's in her room," Ethan said. "Second floor, 201A."

Robert shook his head. "Her bed's empty. And it wasn't a bomb that took out the office. It was a surface-to-air missile, only it wasn't fired from ground level—it was an aerial attack from a dark helicopter with no markings. None of the witnesses were close enough to catch any details. With the way the windows are set up, Miss Benedict is the only person who might've seen the chopper."

Blood roared through Ethan's veins, and he turned and sprinted up the hallway with Robert and Evangeline at his heels, spurred by the knowledge that the TCM conspirators didn't leave witnesses alive.

NICOLE FLICKERED in and out of awareness, sometimes able to process her surroundings, sometimes not.

At first she saw hospital corridors rolling past as her captor wheeled her along. Then she was in an elevator. Another hallway. Then a plain room with gray-green walls and a palpable chill in the air.

The next time she surfaced, she was still in the gray-green room, still strapped to the gurney, but the man in the white lab coat was gone and the room was seriously cold. She shivered, realizing that the room wasn't just somebody-turned-up-the-AC-too-high cold, it was all-the-way-to-igloo freezing.

Like a meat locker, she thought, panic kindling as she twisted her head, trying to get a good look around. She didn't see any dead bodies—she wasn't in the morgue, thank God—but she didn't see much else. The insulated walls of the bare room were painted gray-green, and the shiny white door bore a freezer handle and a small, fogged window. A refrigerator unit bolted to the ceiling above her hummed, blowing cold air.

"Hello?" she said, her words emerging on a puff of vapor as her breath met the chilly air. She raised her voice. "Can anyone hear me?"

The echoes bounced off the walls and door, faint beneath the refrigerator's hum.

Breath clogging in her lungs, she tugged frantically at the straps securing her to the gurney, but succeeded only in pressing her body into the thin mattress beneath her. She felt very small and weak and scared. Worse, she realized she'd stopped shivering, and when she exhaled, the vapor was faint, warning that her core temperature was falling. She was probably only minutes away from hypothermia, maybe an hour away from death.

She sucked in a breath and screamed, "I'm in here! Somebody! Anybody, *get me out of here!*"

Her only response was the hum of the cooling unit.

ETHAN STOOD at the main admittance desk, cold anger pounding in his veins. "She's not in the hospital. The bastards took her."

Robert clasped his shoulder briefly. "We'll find her."

But they both knew that by then it could be too late.

Around them, the admitting area bustled with normal hospital activity, plus the tension of an organized search. All free personnel were on the lookout, and security officers had spread throughout the complex. If she'd been transported somewhere else, though, the effort was useless.

"Call the cops," Ethan said, possibilities flickering through his mind in a gruesome slide show. "You've got friends there. They'll look if you push them."

"Already done," Robert said. "Given that she's the only witness who might have seen—"

"Mr. Moore, Mr. Prescott!" A woman's hail interrupted and Ethan turned to see Dr. Eballa rushing toward them, followed closely by a tall teenager wearing blue scrubs and a volunteer's badge. "I may have something." When she reached the men, she urged the teen forward. "Tell them."

The dark-haired youth looked at a nearby uniformed security officer, flushed and stared at his feet. "There was a guy in the back stairwell."

When he fell silent, Ethan was tempted to grab him and shake the story loose. Instead, he stepped closer and lowered his voice. When he caught the faint scent of pot, he said, "Look, kid. Nobody cares what you were doing or where. Just tell me what you saw."

The teen glanced from Ethan to the guard and back, then mumbled, "Promise?"

"You won't get in trouble for smoking in the stairwell," Ethan said. "At least not this time. After that, you're on your own."

"'Kay." The kid nodded. "So listen, I was in the back stairwell, okay? And this guy came up from the basement wearing a white coat, okay? Only he wasn't a doctor—his clothes were all wrong and he didn't have a badge. Besides, why would a doctor be coming up from the basement? Ain't nothing down there but empty rooms. And he was using a phone, and that's not allowed in here, right?"

Robert interjected, "What did he say?"

"Something like, 'Make up your goddamn mind already.' I didn't hear the rest because I took off before he saw me."

"Are you sure he didn't see you?"

The kid bobbed his head. "Positive."

Ethan turned to Dr. Eballa. "Where are these stairs?"

"I'll take you." As they hurried through the hospital corridors, she said, "He's right, there's not much down there. Mostly empty storage rooms we use as overflow during disasters."

Something chilled inside Ethan. If the white-coated guy in the stairwell had taken Nicole, he might have hidden her down there.

Or he might have dumped her corpse.

He swallowed hard. "What sort of overflow?"

Dr. Eballa pushed through a doorway marked Stairs, then glanced back. "Bodies. Two of the rooms are set up as temporary morgues. We only run the refrigerators when we need the space, though."

They reached the bottom of the stairs and pushed through a set of heavy doors. The corridor was dimly lit. The cement walls were painted a muted green and the floor was white laminate, like much of the rest of the building. But down in the basement, the color scheme didn't seem soothing. It felt swampy. Ominous.

Tension vibrating through every fiber of his being, Ethan shouted, "Nicole? Are you down here?"

When there was no answer, he strode down the corridor, checking doors as the doctor hurried in his wake. The first two rooms were dark and silent. The window of the third was blurred with condensation, and when he felt the door handle, it was cold to the touch.

Robert and a handful of security officers appeared at the far end of the corridor. Ethan shouted, "In here!" He worked the door handle and shoved through, gut tight with apprehension. "Nicole?"

His heart stopped, simply stopped when he saw the motionless figure strapped to a gurney. Dark curls fanned out from a too-pale face, and her lips were the same blue as the thin blanket that covered her body.

"Nicole!" He skidded to her side and yanked at the straps holding her down. When she was free, he felt for her carotid pulse and nearly shuddered at the feel of her corpse-cold flesh. Then, miraculously, he felt a faint flutter beneath his fingertips. Another.

"Move!" Dr. Eballa hustled him aside. "We've got to get her upstairs, stat!"

She turned the gurney toward the door. As she did so, Nicole's eyelids flickered open. She looked around wildly for a moment, then her eyes fixed on Ethan. Her lips formed the words, *Thank you.*

Then she was gone, whisked away by the doctor, who snapped orders about heating blankets, warm-water lavages and an ultrasound. Ethan followed, but Dr. Eballa barred him from cramming into the car with the gurney and the security officers. "Meet us up there, you'll just be in the way." Then she paused, and said, "I'll put a guard on the door, and she'll get the best medical team in the state. God willing, she and the baby will both be fine."

Then the elevator doors slid shut, leaving Ethan behind. He wasn't alone, though. He could hear Robert in the cold room, ordering the security officers to seal the scene and call in the PD, and Evangeline stood in the hallway nearby. He saw the knowledge in her eyes when she said, "Let's head upstairs. You'll want to be there when they've got her stabilized."

It's not what you think, Ethan wanted to say. *I can't be a father.*

Instead, he turned and headed for the stairs, rubbing absently at his chest where an ache had gathered.

Robert emerged and fell into step at his side. "They'll secure the room and I'll make sure the pothead sits down with a sketch artist. I'll put some men on Miss Benedict's room. Once she's conscious, we'll want the artist in with her, too." A flicker of satisfaction crossed his face. "This could be the break we've been waiting for, our chance to nail these bastards."

Instantly furious, Ethan grabbed his boss and slammed him up against the green-painted wall. He crowded close, levered an arm across Robert's throat and got in his face, growling, "Stay the hell away from Nicole. She's not a break in your case, she's not bait, and she's not a pawn in one of your spy games."

The big man didn't give him the satisfaction of struggling. He merely narrowed his eyes. "Then what is she?"

Ethan didn't hesitate, knowing the lie was a necessary evil. "She's mine."

Chapter Four

Evangeline arrived in time to see Ethan release her husband and stalk off, climbing the stairs two at a time.

Robert muttered a curse and smoothed his shirt cuffs even though the garment was hopelessly wrinkled and stained. The small, fastidious detail reminded her of the man she'd fallen in love with seven years earlier, back when she'd been with the FBI and Robert had been trying to get PPS off the ground. He'd helped her find the truth about her parents' deaths, and he'd changed her life by bringing her into his business and his world—or so she'd thought. These days, it was all too clear that he'd let her in only so far, keeping other pieces of himself hidden away.

Now he turned to her, his expression dark

and complicated. "Were you coming to rescue me from Ethan or have him hold me down while you took a few swings?"

"I hadn't decided." She crossed the distance separating them, but kept her attention on the stairs, where Ethan had disappeared. "He's never mentioned Nicole."

"Is that a problem?"

His clipped tone had her glaring. "You think I have something going with Ethan?"

He looked away, a muscle bunching at the corner of his square jaw. "Two years is a long time."

For a split second she thought he might be trying to confess an indiscretion of his own, but there was none of that in his expression when he finally looked back at her. There was only sad resignation, as though he'd already decided the answer for himself.

Anger flared quickly, at him, at the situation, and she snapped, "I know *exactly* how long you were gone, Robert. Worse, thanks to exactly one stinking phone call, I knew you were alive and hiding out. Do you have any idea—" She broke off and gritted her teeth. "Never mind. We've been around this barn a few times already. I hate that you shut me out rather than trusting me to help, and you figure I should be grateful because everything you did was for my own good, to keep me safe. We're at an impasse."

They'd been at loggerheads for weeks now, ever since the first blush of their reunion had worn off. Worse, she wasn't sure there was any way for them to get past this issue. He was a stubborn Brit and she wasn't big on second chances in the absence of a damn good apology, which she had yet to hear.

"I thought you were dead when I first saw your office. I thought—" He broke off and looked away. "I wanted to kill the murdering sod who'd pulled the trigger, followed by the bloody bastard behind it all, and then myself, because I don't want to live another day without you."

Her heart turned over in her chest at the banked violence in his voice, at the raw grief that pressed up into her own throat, the desire to throw herself into his arms, forget the past and only look forward. But early in her life, when she'd lost her childhood to the foster system in the wake of her parents' murders, she'd learned that wanting something wasn't enough, especially in the absence of honesty and trust, so she hardened her heart and said, "Now you know how it feels not to know whether the person you love is alive or dead."

"That's not fair," he said, lowering his voice to a growl when a trio of uniformed police officers emerged from the nearby elevator and headed for the crime scene.

"I know." Evangeline took a step back, away from her husband. "You want things to be like they were before you left, but it doesn't work that way. We've both changed. Hell, I ran your company."

"Is that what this is about? Take the damn company. It's yours, I don't care, just so long as we can get past this and I can have my wife back. So I can have my *life* back."

He cursed and dragged a hand through his salt-and-pepper hair, leaving it spiky. His torn, soiled clothes and disheveled hair made him look sexy and dangerous. Tempting.

Forcing herself to stand her ground, she shook her head. "It's not about the company, Robert, it's about you not trusting me and not letting me be an equal partner in our marriage."

"I trust you," he said, but they both knew

his actions over the past two years said otherwise.

"Come on," she said. "Ever since my name turned up on that list you've been trying to marginalize me."

His eyes glinted with building fury. "I'm not marginalizing you, I'm *protecting* you, and if you don't see the difference, you're—" He clicked his teeth on whatever he'd been about to say, retreating behind the calm, cool facade she thought of as his spy face.

"I'm an FBI-trained agent who neither wants nor needs protection." *And here we are again,* Evangeline thought. *Back at that same old impasse.* She was suddenly tired beyond words and her injured arm throbbed with the beat of her bruised heart. Tears stung her eyelids, a weakness she could ill-afford if she wanted to prove herself to the man who mattered most. Not wanting him to see, she turned away and headed for the stairs. "On that note, I'm going to speak with Ethan's friend. If anything, her abduction says we're not the only ones who think she saw whoever blew up the office."

Evangeline started up the stairs, part of her foolishly hoping Robert would call her back.

When he didn't, a single tear broke free and tracked down her cheek.

WHEN NICOLE regained consciousness this time, she knew exactly where she was—back in her hospital room—and what had happened to her—some guy had grabbed her and tried to turn her into a Popsicle.

What the hell was going on?

She looked for Ethan before she could stop herself, before she could remind herself he'd wanted nothing to do with her or their baby.

Yes, he'd rescued her from the cold room, but then again he was a professional bodyguard; she'd learned that much from the Prescott Personal Securities Web site, along with the fact that he'd mustered out of the military a year or so before he'd joined PPS. A Google search had pulled up little else, which either meant he was relatively baggage-free, or that his baggage wasn't the sort that made it onto the Web.

"And why the hell are you worrying about him when there are more important things going on?" She said the words aloud, partly for emphasis, partly to test her voice, which came out audible but scratchy.

Because, a small voice said inside her, *guy problems are normal. Being nearly killed twice in one day isn't.*

"Do you talk to yourself often?" a female voice asked from the doorway.

Nic winced and turned her head in that direction, and was relieved to see Dr. Eballa rather than…well, just about anyone else who might've been there. At least the doctor was a neutral third party. Because of it, Nic dredged up a smile. "Yeah, as a matter of fact, I do. I just usually check to make sure I'm alone first."

"I think we can forgive the lapse, given the day you've had." The doctor crossed the room and touched her wrist in the same habitual move she'd used before, part reassurance, part pulse check. "How are you feeling?"

"Tired." Nic emphasized the word with a jaw-cracking yawn. "Exhausted, in fact."

"That's not surprising. You should shut down for a bit and let the healing begin."

Nic couldn't keep the wistfulness out of her voice when she said, "Do I have to stay here?"

"As a matter of fact, no," Dr. Eballa said,

surprising her. "Medically, I'm willing to discharge you. But ethically, I need to be sure you'll be safe."

"I don't know—" Nic began, but broke off when a small group appeared in the doorway of her hospital room, with Ethan in the lead.

He announced, "Miss Benedict will be under the protection of Prescott Personal Securities until her attacker has been apprehended."

Nic narrowed her eyes at him. "I appreciate it, but I'm not a client."

When Ethan didn't answer, a fit-looking man in his late fifties stepped forward. His tattered clothes said he'd been in the PPS offices when the missile hit, and his air of authority indicated that he ranked. "I'm Robert Prescott, founder of PPS," he said confirming her guess in a voice that held a faint English accent. He nodded to a blond woman in her late thirties, maybe early forties, who was wearing a sling and a faintly sulky expression. "My wife, Evangeline. You already know Ethan, and these other two are Detectives Riske and Montenegro."

Nic wasn't sure which detective was which: one was a dark-haired woman who walked with an aggressive swagger, the other an older black man with wise eyes and white-frosted hair beneath a Colorado Rockies baseball cap.

"Don't worry, Miss Benedict," Robert Prescott continued. "We'll take care of everything. There's no reason you should suffer because you were in the wrong place at the wrong time." His eyes searched her face. "We're pretty sure that man grabbed you because you were in the elevator at the time of the attack. We're hoping you might remember something that could lead us to the perpetrators."

"I told Ethan before that I don't remember anything about the first attack. I don't even remember being in an elevator," she said slowly. "But I can certainly describe the man who took me out of my room."

Robert nodded. "Then we'll start there."

He stood so the female detective could have his chair. She sat and pulled out a small PDA, which she flipped open and activated with a few touches of a plastic stylus. Then she said, "Detective Shelia Riske, recording an interview with Miss Nicole Benedict." She reeled off the date and location before she focused on

Nic. "Miss Benedict, could you please walk us through what happened earlier today?"

Nic thought for a second, trying to line up her memories in some sort of coherent order. "Ethan had just left my room, and all I wanted to do was go home. I figured if I could make it to the bathroom on my own, I'd be able to convince the doc to spring me. I was halfway across the room when the door opened and a stranger came in…"

ONLY A sheer effort of willpower kept Ethan leaning against the wall as she described what had happened. He wanted to pace and growl, wanted to be out of the hospital, tracking the bastards who'd set their sights on PPS.

Before, he'd been only peripherally involved in the TCM matter. He'd been off on a string of bodyguard assignments during the first stages of the investigation, when Jack Sanders, Mike Lawson and Cameron Morgan, three of the best operatives PPS had in the field, had connected a string of murders to TCM, a mega company run by billionaire Stephen Turner. With Stephen married to Robert Prescott's first wife,

Olivia, and Robert's estranged son, Kyle, working high up in the company, the ties between the conglomerate and Robert— who'd been presumed dead at the time—had seemed too strong for coincidence.

Still, it hadn't really been Ethan's problem. He worked for PPS because Evangeline had recruited him and the lifestyle was a good fit, but he was more of an independent contractor than part of the team. He'd stayed on the edges of the investigation, moving even further into the background when veteran PPS agent John Pinto and rookie Lily Clark brought Robert back from Cuerva Island, where he'd been hiding out and investigating his own death.

Robert returned with solid evidence that his ex-mentor and former business partner, Clive Fuentes, had tried to kill him because he'd gotten too close to one of the lucrative but highly illegal schemes Clive was running under the legitimate business operations at PPS. Robert's investigation had also uncovered a link between Clive and the shell company used to broker the TCM oil-rights-leasing scheme that had led to the murders being investigated at PPS. Clive, however, had disappeared, leaving them unsure of whether he was involved in the attacks, or whether he'd been killed along with a half-dozen of the original oil-rights investors and Lenny, a PPS computer tech.

Lenny's death had hit close to home, but even then Ethan had held himself apart, thinking it wasn't his fight. Rationally, he knew it still wasn't his fight, except that Nicole had been coming to see him when she'd gotten caught up in the danger. That made him responsible.

The child she carried made him doubly responsible, whether he liked it or not.

"Thanks," Detective Riske said, warning him that he'd missed most of Nicole's report. "I think we have what we need." She saved her notes on her handheld and stood. "We'll be in touch to schedule you with our sketch artist, and I'll match your description to some head shots we've got on file. Maybe we'll get lucky."

Judging from her tone, she wasn't holding out too much hope on that, which Ethan had to second. So far, the PPS investigators hadn't gotten any lucky breaks on this investigation. Each time it seemed like they were starting to make headway, things took a turn for the worse.

Detectives Riske and Montenegro exited, talking in the clipped shorthand of longtime partners. That left Ethan, Robert and Evangeline, along with the question of how to keep Nicole safe when every last PPS operative was needed in the field.

"We have a safe house," Robert said, his thoughts clearly paralleling Ethan's. "You can take Miss Benedict there for a few days. Maybe she'll remember something we can use."

"Call me Nicole, please," Nicole said from the hospital bed. With deep purple shadows beneath her eyes and the faint smudge of a bruise on one cheek, she looked too lovely, too vulnerable to be caught up in something as ugly as the TCM mess.

Ethan was tempted to agree to the plan, tempted to hide her away in the safe house and stand guard. But that was emotion talking, not logic.

"You need me on the investigation, not holed up in the safe house," he said flatly. He turned to Evangeline. "Take Nicole to the Vault with you. That way she's safe, and you can run things underground while Robert and I—"

"Don't even finish that statement," Evangeline interrupted, eyes blazing. "And don't think for one second that I'm staying in the Vault while you big, strong men fix everything. Two years ago, Clive Fuentes took the man I loved. I didn't go after him then because I didn't know who was behind it, since somebody—" her eyes flicked to Robert "—wanted to protect me by keeping me in the dark like some idiot child. But not this time. Not ever again. I'm going to be on the front lines of this one, and you two can go to hell."

She stalked out of the room and slammed the door, leaving silence in her wake.

After a moment, Robert let out a breath and glanced at Nicole. "Sorry about that. You two got caught in a bit of a marital crossfire."

"Seemed like more than a bit," Ethan said, rubbing absently at a faint ache in his chest. "Maybe I should go talk to her, apologize or something."

"Don't bother. It's me she really wants to have at." Robert headed for the door.

"Wait!" Nic said quickly. When Robert

turned back, she ordered, "Tell me what's going on here. I deserve to know why someone tried to kill me."

She'd gotten some color back in her cheeks, Ethan noticed, which made him think anger became her. Then again, pretty much everything suited her. She was a lovely woman, through and through, one who'd made him feel—

Nothing, he thought sharply. She'd made him feel nothing because he chose to feel nothing. No strong attachments, no repeat business, no promises. It was better that way.

"Ethan will bring you up to speed," Robert said, voice brooking no argument. "He'll stick with you and keep you safe while you try to remember what you saw from that elevator. It could be the break we need." He glanced at Ethan. "You said it yourself—she's yours."

With that, he turned and exited the hospital room, where the air hung thick with tension.

"Sorry," Ethan said, knowing she deserved far better than she was getting. But that was the point, wasn't it? She—and the baby—deserved better than he was capable of giving.

"There's no need to apologize. You've made your position perfectly clear already," she said coolly. "But since it looks like we're stuck with each other, how about telling me what the hell's going on?" She paused, glanced around and frowned. "On second thought, do you have a car here?"

Unwilling to admit that he'd argued his way onto the ambulance with her, he said, "My Jeep." Robert had arranged to have it driven to the hospital once the immediate panic had settled down.

She sat up and swung her legs over the side of the bed, giving him a serious eyeful of bare thigh before she yanked the blanket off the bed and draped it around herself, toga-style.

Ethan scowled. "Don't even think you're leaving. You've got a concussion."

"And you were trained as a medic," she shot back, surprising him. "I'll be fine. Dr. Eballa said I could leave." Then she looked at him, a hint of vulnerability creeping into her eyes. "Look, Ethan. The situation stinks for both of us, but it'll stink a whole lot less for me once I get out of here. I want to be in my apartment, wearing real clothes and hunkered down under my afghan, okay? And if that makes me terminally lame, then so be it."

"You're not lame," Ethan said softly, "but you can't go home. They knew your name and your hospital room number. I guarantee they know where you live."

"Oh. Hell." She paled, but pressed her lips together resolutely and nodded. "You're right. Of course you're right. But I don't want to go to your place, and I'm not going to that vault thing Robert was talking about. I want neutral territory."

"I can respect that." Heck, it's what he would've insisted on in her situation. "A hotel, then." When her eyes sharpened, he was reminded of the other time they'd been in a hotel room together. Ignoring the hard, hot stab that buried itself in his gut, he held up a hand. "Separate rooms with a connecting door. Deal?"

She looked at him for a long moment. Then she nodded. "Deal."

EXHAUSTION beat through every fiber of Nic's body, but pride had her shaking off Ethan's offer of help and stalking to his late-model Jeep under her own power. She even managed not to whimper as she climbed into the passenger's side and strapped herself into the bucket seat, but it was a close call. God, she was tired. And sore. And confused.

Once they were on the night-darkened road, she glanced over at his set profile, visible in the glow of dashboard indicators and the flicker of oncoming headlights. "Okay, give me the short version. I'm not sure I can stay awake for anything longer than that."

He nodded, but kept his attention on the road when he began. "It all starts with a man named Clive Fuentes. He was Robert's mentor back in the day, when Robert was British intelligence at MI6 and Clive was working for their Spanish counterpart, IR6. After both of them retired, they hooked back up here in the States and decided to go into the personal security business together. At the time it seemed like a fortuitous coincidence. Now it looks like Clive was trolling for an aboveboard partner to hide some seriously dirty dealings. When Robert started looking too closely, Clive arranged for him to die in a plane crash. That was two years ago."

Surprise skittered through her, along with new unease at the realization she'd stumbled into something far bigger than she'd suspected. Somehow, the air strike and the incident at the hospital had seemed, if not spur of the moment, then not fully planned out. This new information made the situation seem far more complicated, far more dangerous, which had her feeling a faint hitch of relief when he took the next side street and she realized he was doubling back on their track and keeping a sharp eye on the rearview mirror.

She might not be totally comfortable with him, but she had to admit she felt better knowing she had a trained bodyguard on her side.

"Go on," she urged.

He glanced at her, and then back at the road before he said, "Obviously, Robert didn't die in the crash. He went into hiding, figuring that was the best way to protect Evangeline from whoever was after him."

"I take it she hasn't forgiven him for that move yet," Nic said, remembering the scene in her hospital room.

"That's putting it mildly," Ethan agreed.

"Once he'd tracked the crash and various dirty business dealings back to Clive, Robert contacted PPS, which Evangeline had kept up and running while he was gone. With the help of a couple of our operatives, he was able to transfer a big chunk of Clive's money out of an offshore account. When that didn't flush Clive out of hiding, Robert came home. That was last month. Since then, we've been doing our best to locate Clive, but he's disappeared."

Nic nodded slowly. "If this Clive is trying to protect his own butt by killing Robert, though, why the air strike at the office building? That was pretty dramatic."

"It's more complicated than that." Ethan glanced at her, eyes deadly serious. "Did you follow any of the news surrounding Nick Warner's death?"

She shook her head. "I've seen his movies, sure. And I knew he'd been killed. It was a stalker, right?"

"That's how the PR people spun it," Ethan said. "Truth is, his death, and at least six others seem to be connected to an illegal and very big-money oil-rights pyramid scheme. PPS got involved because one of our agents was guarding Warner's wife the night he was killed, and wound up with an encrypted disk and the name of the next victim. One thing led to another and now we're all neck-deep in this mess. Most of the evidence points back to a company called Tri Corp. Media, but we seem to have hit a dead end there. The head honcho, Stephen Turner, is clean. His son Peter was one of the major players in the scheme, but he was taken out of the action a couple of months ago, and things have kept getting worse since." He grimaced. "The bastards are focused on PPS now. They even took out one of our techs. Lenny. Nice kid."

Nic pressed her fingertips to her eyes, trying to slow the spinning in her brain. "So let me get this straight. There are two sets of people who want to destroy PPS?"

"Yes and no. Thing is, the pyramid scheme was funneled through the same shell company Clive was using—Kingston Trust." He paused. "What we don't know yet is whether Clive was working with Peter to run the whole show, or if he was just an investor of some sort, one who didn't make it onto the list for some reason."

"List?" Nic's head was buzzing with all the information, but she was rapidly becoming convinced that leaving the hospital and *not* going back to her apartment were both very good decisions. This whole thing was way bigger than she'd expected.

"We got our hands on a computerized list of the Kingston Trust investors, including all of the dead men, in order of death, with Evangeline's name at the bottom." There was a low burn of anger in Ethan's voice now, one that suggested his relationship with Robert's wife went deeper than boss-employee.

The realization jarred Nic with conflicting emotions—both empathy and jealousy for a woman she'd barely met. "I take it she never invested in Kingston Trust."

"No. It's a hit list. And I hate to say it, but it's a safe bet she's not the last one on it anymore. Not after what happened today."

"What do you—" Nic broke off abruptly when she realized there was a good chance her name had been added to the list because she'd been in the wrong elevator at the wrong time and had seen something that could lead PPS and the cops to the killers. Something she couldn't remember.

She shivered and looked out the window as Ethan signaled and pulled into the neon-lit parking area outside of one of the many hotels clustered near the Denver International Airport.

He rolled to a stop, threw the transmission into Park and glanced at her. "This okay?"

"As tired as I am right now, it could be a Shingle Roof Inn with no roof and I wouldn't complain."

"Good." He climbed down from the driver's side, and she was shaky enough to wait until he opened her door and helped her down. But when they were just shy of the hotel entrance, he lifted a hand to a passing cab. When the vehicle pulled over, he opened the door and gestured her in, crowding her with his big body as he slid in after her. "The Crowne, please."

"That's back the way we came," Nic protested, then realized what he was up to. "Oh."

He nodded and said in an undertone, "It's just a precaution, in case I wasn't as careful as I thought, or they have the Jeep bugged."

She exhaled and felt tears press as the day's events began to catch up with her. "Thanks. I'm glad… I appreciate what you're doing for me."

"I'm a bodyguard," he said simply.

"Right," Nic said, letting her head fall back against the seat, unaccountably disappointed.

She didn't remember falling asleep, but the next thing she knew, Ethan was nudging her awake. "We're here. Can you make it a little farther?"

"Of course." She struggled up, feeling every bruise and ache as she followed Ethan into the hotel, practically dozing on her feet while he rented them connecting rooms. He guided her onto the elevators and off at the correct floor, then swiped the key card and held open the door to her room.

"You'll be safe in here. Room service is sending up a wrapped sandwich and a couple of bottles of water. I'm right next door if you need anything."

"Thanks." She looked up at him, fatigue making her feel so fragile she might shatter from it. "Thanks for everything. I know this wasn't what you wanted to—"

He touched a finger to her lips. "Turn it off for a few hours. We'll deal with everything else tomorrow."

They stood like that for a heartbeat, with

his fingertip just grazing her lower lip, bringing a shimmer of contact and awareness to her midsection.

He stepped back before she could react. "Sorry. See you in the morning."

He let the door swing shut between them. Moments later, the electronic lock engaged.

"Damn it." Nic pressed her lips together, trying not to feel a hum of warmth at the place he'd just touched. "Just damn it."

She didn't bother showering or finger-brushing her teeth, or even undressing. She just toed off her shoes and headed straight for the king-sized bed that dominated the high-end hotel room. She was so tired that the soft mattress felt like a cloud, the cotton comforter like the finest silk.

She was asleep within minutes.

Her dreams teemed with dark, amorphous images and the sensation of falling, of suffocating. Then she *was* suffocating.

She jolted awake on a muffled scream with her heart hammering in her chest and her breath locked in her lungs. A man's weight pressed her into the mattress as he straddled her, his knees pinning her arms at her sides and his hand covering her mouth and nose.

He didn't speak, didn't react to her struggles except to tighten his legs at her sides. He simply pressed down and waited for her to die.

Chapter Five

Ethan was on his feet and across the hotel room before he knew he was awake. Not questioning the response or the battle-ready adrenaline buzz, he yanked open the connecting door.

A man's dark shadow leapt off the bed and fled for the hallway door. Ethan roared and lunged in pursuit, nearly going down when the bastard yanked a desk chair into his path. The stumble cost him precious seconds, and by the time he'd regained his balance, the man was out the door and running down the hall.

Ethan bolted after him, but then stopped, knowing that his responsibility to his protectee outweighed the needs of the PPS investigation. He was a bodyguard first, a teammate second.

"Nicole!" He pushed back through the door and slapped at the light switch just inside the room. Bulbs flared to life, showing her lying deathly still on the rumpled bed.

With a wordless cry, Ethan lunged toward her, then stopped, knees locking when he looked down and her image was overlain with another, that of a lighter-haired woman with an aquiline nose and a sprinkle of freckles on her cheeks, lying on rain-slicked pavement, her eyes open and staring.

"No!" Ethan reached for Nicole, intending to nudge her, shake her, whatever it took to bring her back. Then he stopped and stood, paralyzed with history, and with the knowledge that the bastards had gotten past him to hurt his protectee. To hurt Nicole.

Logic, not knee-jerk reaction, he reminded himself. *Work it through. What's the first step, and what are the risks?*

His mind was a blank, his old training gone in an instant. There was no sign of blood, but her eyes were closed, her skin was sallow and her breath hitched slightly as she exhaled. Had she aggravated the concussion? Had she—

Her eyelids fluttered, bringing a sharp slap

of relief. Ethan leaned over her. "Nicole? Can you hear me?"

She murmured something low and sweet and incomprehensible. Moments later she frowned and shifted, then her eyes flew open and she gasped, lifting her hands to her throat and struggling up on the bed until she was pressed up against the headboard, looking around with her eyes wild and her mouth open in a silent scream.

"You're okay," Ethan said quickly, still not daring to touch her. "He's gone. You're fine." He hoped. He couldn't believe the bastard had found them, couldn't believe he'd underestimated how important they considered Nicole.

He had only himself to blame for not burying their trail more effectively. He'd been too casual with her protection. In trying to buffer himself against her presence, and the knowledge of the child she carried, he'd nearly let her be killed.

"God." Nicole touched her throat, where the skin was still red from the pressure of her attacker's hands. "That was…" She trailed off, then swallowed with a wince. She shifted on the bed and winced again, this time touching her waist, where the bottom layer of her tattered sweater-shirt combo was still halfway tucked into her jeans. "Something doesn't feel right."

"Lie down," Ethan ordered immediately. "I'll call Dr. Eballa."

"No!" she said quickly, sitting all the way up and clasping her hands together in front of herself as if in protection. "No, please. No more ambulances, no more hospitals. It was nothing. Probably just a pulled muscle or something."

"Or it could be the baby," Ethan countered, automatically reaching into his pocket for his cell, only to realize he didn't have his phone. Or pockets. He'd gone to bed in his boxers and nothing else, and he was suddenly far too conscious of his near nudity. He headed for the connecting door. "We're getting out of here as soon as I'm dressed, in case anyone else comes looking for you."

In his own room, he pulled on his cargo pants and shirt, shoved his fully-licensed Beretta 9 mm into his waistband and dug out his cell phone. He made a few calls, and by the time he headed back to her room, he'd come up with what ought to be a workable plan to get her checked out without another hospital visit.

"Here's the deal. We're going to—" He broke off when he found her sitting on the edge of the bed with her face in her hands. "Aw, hell." He dropped down to sit beside her, his weight causing the mattress to dip, urging her closer to his side. He slung an arm around her, intending it as a friendly, supportive gesture. "It's going to be okay, Nicole."

"Nic," she mumbled miserably into her hands. "My friends call me Nic."

Are we friends? he wanted to ask, but didn't because he knew they weren't. They were both more and less than friends, two strangers linked by a life created by a point-oh-one percent error factor in the fine print of the condom package. The thought—or maybe the feel of her pressed against his side—reminded him of their night together, of the unexpected flash and flame they'd created together. The echoes of that night warmed him even as a different sort of urgency beat beneath his skin, as his instincts warned that they needed to get moving.

Instead, he let his cheek rest on the top of

her head. "Nic, then. And don't worry, I'm not going anywhere until we get Clive Fuentes *and* those bastards at TCM."

Problem was, the TCM investigation was heading into month six. What if it took another six months for them to get things under control? By then, Nic would be close to eight and a half months, and—

His thoughts veered away from the sudden image of her fully pregnant, her cheeks and belly round with it.

"I called Dr. Eballa," he said, standing abruptly and holding out a hand to help her up. "She'll meet us at my condo."

His condo. His refuge, where he'd never brought a protectee before. Never brought a woman before.

Nicole frowned. "Won't they be watching your place?"

"They're in for some nasty surprises if they try anything. Cam, one of the PPS operatives, is a whiz with security and he hooked me up with all the latest. We'll be safe there for an hour or so." Which was about how long it would take her attacker to scramble the helicopter for an aerial attack, which not even Cam's finest devices could hold out against.

"And after that?"

"One thing at a time," he said, and led her out of her room and through the hotel with his 9 mm at the ready.

HIS CONDO, half of a large craftsman-style home the previous owners had inexplicably split into a two-family, was less than twenty minutes from the airport hotel cluster. At barely 4:00 a.m. near the end of summer, the Denver streets were quiet, making him feel exposed and too obvious as he pulled into the driveway on his side of the house.

A small LED light on the mailbox flicked from red to green and back to red as the device recognized the transponder in his Jeep. Should another, unidentified vehicle pass through, two hidden cameras would activate and a chime would sound in the house, warning of company. A series of motion detectors around the house provided a second line of defense, flicking on lights as Ethan and Nicole emerged from the Jeep and he led her around to the side entrance. There, he pressed his thumb to a glossy pad for identification, and when his print was accepted, keyed in an alphanumeric password that changed on a weekly basis.

"Impressive," Nic said from beside him. "I take it you've had to hide people here before?"

"The guys were working on a new system and needed a guinea pig." Ethan unlocked the door with a coded key and ushered her through. "Evangeline volunteered me."

As he locked the door behind them, he shrugged against the tension that gathered in his shoulders. When he turned back, he found her poised at the entrance to his main room, backlit by the lamps that had come on when he'd keyed through the security system.

He'd filled his place with mission-style furniture that complemented the clean lines and carved embellishments of the town-house, and he'd covered the windows with slatted wood blinds that matched the polished hardwood floors. He'd left the other stuff to a decorator who'd been another of Evangeline's projects—a wispy twenty-something with a soft voice and a prison tattoo on the back of one hand—and had wound up with upholstery, rugs and curtains all in shades of green and tan, with an occasional pop of royal-blue. It was all clean and linear, and he kept it pin-neat. That part was only rational, because he never knew when he'd be leaving for an assignment, and there was nothing worse than coming home to chaos.

Except, he realized with a start, this time he'd brought the chaos home with him.

Nic's eyes were shadowed with questions and fears as she looked at him. He expected her to ask for reassurance.

Instead, she grimaced. "I'm sorry about this, Ethan. I know babysitting me isn't exactly what you had planned for the week."

Deciding they could either tiptoe around the issue or face it head-on, he said, "I expect being a single mom wasn't what you'd planned for your next eighteen years or so, either."

She smiled faintly and lifted one shoulder. "Maybe. But it was way more fun than going to a sperm bank."

That startled a laugh out of him. He crossed to her and took her hands to give them a friendly squeeze. Then he looked at her for a long moment, seeing how she didn't really fit among his things, and shook his head. "This would be a whole lot easier if I didn't like you."

Her smile went crooked. "Same goes."

And though they both knew this wasn't the right situation and they weren't the right couple, it felt absolutely, positively right to Ethan when he leaned down and kissed her.

NIC SAW the change in his eyes, saw that he gave her plenty of time to back off, but her instincts for self-preservation lost the battle.

She and Ethan had been lovers and she carried his child. Why not kiss him? If nothing else, she could prove to herself that the things she'd felt that night had been amplified by her emotions and one drink too many. There was no way it could be as good as she remembered.

Except it was.

The moment their lips touched, her mind blanked to everything but the flare of heat that came with the first moment of contact, when he hesitated ever so slightly, as though waiting for her to pull away. Instead, she leaned in and opened to him, helpless to stop the faint gasp that escaped when their tongues touched, tentatively at first and then with growing pressure, increasing heat and need.

She slid her arms around his neck and rose

up on her tiptoes to align their mouths more surely as the kiss grew wetter, hotter, more demanding. Her nipples tightened and need spiked deep in her belly, sharp and fierce. She strained closer to him even as some small part of her brain, the part that hadn't fully short-circuited at the feel of his hard muscles and the close-clipped hair beneath her fingertips, registered a pang of fear.

It wasn't a false memory. The feelings were real. The need was real, but Ethan had made it clear he couldn't give her any more than he already had.

As though realizing the same thing, he broke the kiss and pressed his lips to her forehead, letting them linger there while they breathed together, their rhythms perfectly in tune. "I'm sorry," he said, voice rough. "We shouldn't do this."

The evidence of his desire was a good, hard lump pressing into her, one that had her rubbing against him to feel the answering flare within, the answering burn of her blood. "Probably not," she said, but she didn't care, which was a revelation.

Nic had never been particularly sexual or spontaneous, which was why Jonah had looked elsewhere for excitement. She was steady and reliable, not exciting and fun. Except, it appeared, with this man. With Ethan.

"This is crazy," he said, barely getting the words out before he was kissing her again.

"Crazy," she agreed as a bubble of excitement worked its way up from her belly and pressed in her throat, and her head spun with the mad heat of it all, the joy of feeling her body respond. It had been a long time since she'd felt like this, if ever. She grinned as she unlinked her hands from around his neck and let them slide down to rest at his waist. Through the warm material of his shirt, she felt the taut muscles of his abdomen clench at her touch. "Insane."

She leaned into him and he reached down for her, and they met halfway. There was no hesitation this time, no more discussion. Everything around them might be incomprehensible, but this made sense, she thought. This was right. It was real.

He slanted his mouth across hers and his fingers went to work on the clothes she'd slept in, the clothes she'd nearly died in. Moments later, his fingers touched the bare skin of her waist, sending pinprick lightning sizzles through her body. She murmured his name against his lips and crowded close, tugging his shirt from his waistband and sliding her hands up to the hard planes of his chest, where a smattering of hair dusted his warm, masculine skin.

Her head spun, the room spun, but not because of the fading effects of the concussion. It was because of Ethan. Only Ethan.

Still kissing her, he walked them through his living room until they bumped into a couch. She had a brief impression of polished wood and lots of masculine greens and browns, and then they dropped to the couch in perfect accord. He came down atop her, bracing himself not to crush her with his full weight while he shifted, pulled a deadly looking gun from his waistband, and set it on a nearby end table with an ominous clunk.

The gesture was a cold splash of reality, a reminder of the danger stalking her. But they were safe in Ethan's home, Nic knew, letting the feeling of security warm her as she nestled against him. Kissed him. Touched him. Within moments, they were straining together, male against female, hard against soft. The madness rocketed through her, the need to feel him, caress him, sink herself into him and surround him all at once.

This was what had been missing with Jonah, she realized. This was what she'd come to Denver to find. Not a father for her child, but a man to complete her as a woman. Knowing it, glorying in it, she went to work at his belt and zipper, then slid one hand into the warm nest within and curled her fingers around his pulsing length, startling a hiss out of him.

He drew back and looked down at her, his eyes dark with passion and wild with need. "Nicole."

That was all he said, just her name, but it was enough, an acknowledgment that they weren't strangers this time, weren't half-drunk and emotional. This time, they would become lovers because they wanted to, because they craved the slap of flesh and the taste of one another and the musk they created together.

Feeling her heart drum in her chest, she squeezed him lightly, intimately. He rolled to his side so they could face each other and kiss while he tugged at her shirt, at her pants, loosening and peeling away layers until she was open to his touch, until her nipples peaked and sensation spun nearly out of control. He kissed her face, her neck, her upper chest as his fingers toyed lightly with her breasts, then traced lower down, to where her open pants allowed access. He dipped his finger beneath the elastic of her panties, then lower, where she felt wet and hot and ready to explode.

Then she *was* exploding, climaxing from little more than the brush of his fingertip across her exquisitely sensitized flesh.

She cried his name and bowed against him, moaning when he rubbed firmly, prolonging the waves of pleasure that began at that spot and radiated outward, grabbing and letting go in pulsations that seemed to go on forever.

Ethan groaned deep in his chest and shuddered as she came, his hard flesh jerking near to completion, but not quite there, which excited her even more, knowing he was still hard for her, still needing her.

Her pleasure drained but didn't fade, leveling off, poised on another heart-drumming cliff, one that needed him inside her to take flight.

She opened her eyes and found his face very near hers, his eyes very brown and tinged with a softer emotion than she'd seen before. "Nicole," he said softly, raising a hand to her face and brushing a feather-light touch across her cheek. "I—"

A faint chime sounded in the room. Ethan froze against her for a split second, then lunged off the couch.

He grabbed the gun off the end table and racked the slide, the deadly click echoing loudly in the room as he crossed it in three quick strides. He stood off to one side of the door as he tapped a sequence on a small keypad, bringing a tiny video monitor to life.

With his untucked shirt hanging open and his pants gaping across his hips, he should have looked vulnerable. Instead, he looked deadly dangerous, and the realization reminded Nic just how little she knew about him.

"Hell." He exhaled a long breath and slid the safety, then fastened his pants and shoved the gun into his waistband before he glanced at Nic, expression unreadable. "It's Dr. Eballa."

"Oh." Blood running high into her cheeks,

Nic stood and turned away to pull her clothing into place, flustered by the chill realization that she'd nearly done it again, nearly chucked caution in favor of sensation. When she turned back to him, she thought she saw the same knowledge in his dark eyes. She exhaled and said, "What is it about us that makes the wrong thing feel so right?"

He grimaced. "I wish I knew." Then he opened the door and ushered in Dr. Eballa, who was neatly dressed in street clothes with her hair slicked back in a ponytail, but still carried sleep in her eyes. Without breaking stride, he led them across the large main room and up a flight of polished wood stairs to a large bedroom that took up the entire second floor. He clicked on the lights and waved them through. "I'll be downstairs so you two can have some privacy."

That left Nic standing just inside his bedroom; it was done in the same greens and browns and polished wood, and was dominated by a huge, neatly made four-poster bed. A door stood open at the far end of the long, narrow space, offering a glimpse of a lavish-looking bathroom. Similar to downstairs, the space was sparsely though tastefully decorated, and almost ruthlessly neat. Up in the bedroom, though, the air held a hint of the man, a faint mix of soap and after-shave, and the solid, masculine flavor of Ethan himself.

In the aftermath of what had happened on the couch, Nic felt beyond awkward at being in his bedroom. She glanced at the doctor. "I'm sorry he dragged you out here. I'm fine." Her fingers drifted down to her belly, where lingering heat coexisted with her growing child. "We're fine."

Which made her wonder whether the pregnancy had jump-started her hormones, or vice versa? With Ethan, it seemed, all bets were off.

The doctor smiled faintly. "I believe you. But let's take a look, anyway."

Her exam was quick but thorough, and at the end she nodded. "You're right. You're both fine, physically. As for the other stuff…" She tilted her head. "I'm an excellent listener, if you want to talk."

Nic was a private person, usually keeping to herself even amongst her friends at the school. But the past thirty hours—and the ten weeks preceding—had been anything but usual, and she found herself sinking down to the edge of the bed and dropping her head into her hands. "Where do I start?"

THE EXAM probably only took thirty minutes, but Ethan felt as if he'd spent hours pacing from the kitchen to the video monitor beside the door and back. He could've tried to pretend he was on the lookout for danger, but that would've been a lie and he tried very hard not to lie to himself. Not anymore.

"That was unfair to her," he said aloud. "You should learn to keep your lips to yourself."

Except it wasn't as though he had a history of indiscretions. Hell, there'd only been a few women since Caro, and they'd all been logical choices, friend-of-a-friend hookups who'd been easy to spend time with and equally easy to walk away from a few dates later with no hard feelings on either side, just two people who didn't quite fit.

Well, he and Nic didn't fit either. She was hearth and home and he was… Well, he was what he was. And even if they might've been able to do the no-hard-feelings thing—and he had no doubt he would've enjoyed spending that time—her pregnancy complicated things all to high hell.

A man just didn't hook up with a mother-to-be unless he meant it. He just didn't.

Or rather, Ethan thought, pinching the bridge of his nose in frustration, in recrimination, *he shouldn't.*

Hearing a set of footsteps on the stairs, he straightened away from the front door and crossed the living room to meet Dr. Eballa. "How is she?"

She gave him a long look before she said, "Physically, they're *both* fine." The stress on the word was a subtle condemnation. "Emotionally, Nicole is stressed and strung out, and she could use a little kindness."

Ethan nodded. "I know." But as he walked the doctor to her vehicle and reset the security system once she'd pulled away, her words echoed in his head.

He would've handled the bodyguard thing differently if Nic had been a client or a friend. He would've explained the situation better and tried to make matters easier on her instead of confusing things with personal issues that had no business on a protection detail.

When he returned to the house, he found her sitting on the couch where they'd been groping each other not an hour earlier. But there was none of that in her expression, which held only determination when she said, "I know I said I wanted us on neutral ground, but that's stupid, isn't it? I'm endangering both of us by insisting on being out in the open, and I'm forcing you to waste your energy protecting me when you should be helping the others find Clive Fuentes and figure out how he's connected to the murders."

Ethan took a step toward her, then stopped. The hollow, scared look in her eyes made him want to tell her everything was going to be okay, but he never made a promise he wasn't certain he could keep. Instead, he said, "You're right, but it's not your fault. I should've insisted on going to the Vault in the first place."

She firmed her chin and nodded. "We both made the mistake, but we can fix it." She stood and stalked past him. "Let's go."

Chapter Six

Robert's carry-on felt as though it weighed a ton and his bones ached as he joined the line of passengers waiting to board the flight to Madrid. It wasn't age dragging him down, or exhaustion, though. It was disappointment, and the knowledge that Evangeline wasn't willing to forgive him for the things he'd done, wasn't willing to understand that he'd done them to keep her safe.

When he'd been stuck in hiding, missing her with every fiber of himself, he'd found a measure of contentment, even pride, in the knowledge that he was protecting the woman he loved. She knew he was alive, he'd rationalized. She'd wait for him, and welcome him back with open arms.

And she had. Then she'd stepped back and all but kicked him in the gut, making it into an issue of trust, a marital test that he'd failed.

"Madrid?" her voice said in his ear, and for a moment he thought the sound was his subconscious chastising him for sneaking out before she awoke.

Then he realized he wasn't imagining her. She was standing right behind him in line.

And she was furious.

His heart ached in his chest as he reached out and touched her face, tracing the curve of her cheek with his fingertip. "I don't want to fight, Evie."

She grabbed his wrist, and he half expected her to push his hand away. Instead, she tightened her fingers and pressed her palm to his cheek. "Me neither. I wanted to tell you to be careful."

Which only made him feel worse as the line crept toward the desk, where attendants were double-checking passports and tickets. He tried for a smile and nodded to the ticket envelope poking out of her coat pocket. "Going somewhere?"

"I bought the cheapest international flight I could find, so I could get onto the concourse. They almost stopped me for a search because I didn't have luggage, but I guess I'm not the first person who ever decided to hit Cancun on a whim." She shrugged, trying for nonchalance even as her eyes filmed with tears. "The thing is, the last time you snuck off before dawn to catch a plane, you didn't come home."

Robert's breath whooshed out on a sucker punch of guilt. "Oh, hell. Evie, I'm sorry."

"It's okay." She shrugged again, a jerky motion that let him know just how not okay she was. "I'm a big girl. It just…hit me, you know? When I woke up this morning and you were gone, I freaked. I thought I was past all that, but I guess I'm not." She looked away from him, a faint blush staining her porcelain skin. "Sorry."

"No," he said urgently. "Don't be." He pulled them both out of line, moving into the lee of a wide pillar beyond the gate area. He dropped his carry-on so he could take both of her hands as he searched for the words. "I didn't think, I just…" He paused as her brimming tears prompted an unwelcome realization. "I haven't been part of an 'us' for so long, I'm out of the habit of thinking about anyone but myself. I didn't want a scene, so when I got the call that Cameron got a line on Clive, I buggered off before you woke up, not stopping to think how you'd feel." He squeezed her hands. "I'm so sorry."

"But you're not going to ask me to go along with you."

He shifted uncomfortably. "I can't."

"You won't," she countered, but her shoulders slumped. "And even if you did, I need to stay here. The support staffers don't know their way around the Vault, which means there's going to be a burn-in period."

When she pulled away, he let her go. "We need to finish this," he said. "We need to take down Clive and whoever else is involved in the attacks. When we do, we'll go away for a few weeks, someplace we can talk. I promise."

Her smile turned sad. "I think we've gone beyond talking at this point, Robert." Before he could ask what she meant by that, she'd leaned up on her tiptoes and pressed a cool, chaste kiss to his lips. "Fly safe and call me when you land."

Then she was leaving, walking away from him with those swinging, unhurried strides that covered more ground than it looked like they should.

When he called her name, she didn't look back.

NIC SUPPRESSED a shiver as Ethan drove his Jeep through a concealing screen of brush into an angular tunnel formed of poured cement. Cut into a hillside that looked like every other hillside in the area, the access had been invisible until they were practically on top of it. The tunnel ran a few hundred feet, then opened up into a shallow vehicle bay that led to an armored door. Staring at the door, Nic said, "It's a vault, all right."

And it felt as though once they went in, they were never coming back out.

"Evangeline told me it was a bomb shelter of some sort." Ethan popped his seat belt and slid out of the Jeep. "Wait here while I buzz us through."

He crossed to a hardwired unit bolted beside the door. When he pressed his palms on a flat screen, then bent close and stared into an optical eye, Nic realized it was a sophisticated ID system.

The realization loosened something inside her, letting her know that she was more worried about the danger than she'd let on, even to herself.

"We'll be safe here," she said aloud, trying to believe the words as Ethan returned to the Jeep.

"Evangeline is going to meet us inside," he said. He swung back into the vehicle and popped it into gear while the armored door parted at the center, grinding back into recessed pockets and revealing another tunnel.

Ethan sent the Jeep down the second tunnel, which descended at a shallow angle. Behind them, the armored doors groaned back into place.

For no good reason, something inside Nic whispered, *Abandon hope all ye who enter here,* making her shiver. Ethan glanced over but didn't comment. Moments later, the tunnel opened up to a startlingly normal-looking parking garage. A dozen other vehicles were parked in a cluster, and Ethan added his Jeep to the end of a row before turning to her. "It's going to be okay, Nicole. Nobody will bother you here."

"I know," she said, and she knew they

weren't just talking about the people trying to kill her.

He nodded as though they'd just agreed to far more than had been said aloud. "Come on. Let's get you settled."

She trailed him across the garage to a high cement wall with a small inset door along with another security station. He went through the same palm-and-eye-scan routine and the door swung inward, revealing another, smaller cement corridor. The walls were covered with a layer of ivory paint, and a no-nonsense brown carpet lined the floor.

Ethan stepped aside and gestured her through. "After you."

He steered her down one long corridor and up another, where they began to see signs of life. Three people wearing jeans and T-shirts were clustered around a bank of laptops and a snarl of cables in one room opening off the hallway. In the next, a dark-haired woman barked into a landline phone, speaking fluent Spanish.

"There's no wireless signal down here," Ethan said, turning them down another corridor, where the doors were more regularly spaced and numbered, and had touch pads that served as keys. "No cell phone signal, and all the computer stuff is hardwired."

"You've been here before?"

He shook his head. "Evangeline gave us a quick briefing on what to expect, along with maps of the facility and our room assignments. This one's yours." He tapped a quick sequence onto the keypad and the door unlocked with a click. "All the doors are coded to 1234. Evangeline decided to keep it simple, since there's so few of us, and we're all working toward the same goal."

He pushed open the door, revealing a room that was maybe ten feet square, with no windows or bathroom. A narrow bed rested against one wall, made with utilitarian neatness and sharply folded corners, and a small desk was pushed against the opposite wall, bare save for a lamp. The walls were painted that same ivory-cream color, and the short, coarse carpeting was of the same indeterminate gray-brown as the hallway.

Ethan grimaced. "Sorry. Evangeline warned me that the accommodations were pretty sparse. Guess she wasn't kidding."

"It's fine," Nic said, but a hard lump

gathered in her throat, a sharp yearning for her multicolored afghan and the piles of pillows that formed drifts on her sofa and bed at home. "Just like camping."

Ethan snorted. "You camp at federal penitentiaries often?" He paused, then glanced over his shoulder at the hallway. "I need to meet with the team and get up to speed, but I'll check on you in a few hours. The mess hall is down the corridor to your left, the bathrooms are clearly marked, and there's a TV in the lounge off the mess. If you need anything, track down our receptionist, Angel—she's a sweetheart under the black makeup and general incompetence. I'll let her know that you'll need a computer and a landline phone in here." His eyes went serious, and his voice dropped a notch. "If you call anyone, just promise me you won't tell them where you are, not even a hint. The signals are scrambled to hell and back, so there's no way the call could be traced, but we have to assume that whoever is after you, whether it's Clive or TCM or both, is very smart. Smart enough to take a few clues and put them together into a location."

Nic stifled the shiver and nodded. "Gotcha.

No hints or clues. I appreciate the access, though. I've got some serious scrambling to do pulling together funding for my pet project."

"Biofuel."

Surprised and foolishly pleased that he'd remembered, Nic nodded. "That's right. My sponsor backed out, school starts next month, and…" She trailed off, realizing that nothing was the same as it had been. There was no guarantee she'd be safe when classes started, and what was she going to do about that? Even if Ethan and his team managed to negate the danger, there was still the question of what she was going to do next spring as her due date approached.

Never mind the year after that, when she'd have a baby, but no husband or family support.

Suddenly, fears that had been submerged by the immediate danger flared to the fore-front of her mind. As much as she wanted the baby, with or without Ethan's involvement, she was equally worried about how the next year—heck, the next fifteen or twenty years—would play out.

"Hey," Ethan said, correctly interpreting

her wince. "I meant what I said before. I'll help with the finances. I make a good living."

She looked away. "Go to your meeting. When you get a chance, let me know what I can do to help, okay? It'll only take me an hour or so make the calls I need to for the biofuel project. After that, I'll go nutty if I'm stuck in here with nothing but online solitaire to keep me company."

He nodded and smiled, though the expression didn't make it to his eyes. "Will do."

She let the door swing shut in his wake, closing out the drab hallway. When she sank to the narrow bed, she found it springier and more comfortable than she'd expected, and felt the tired ache in her bones and behind her eyelids drawing her down. She collapsed onto her side and closed her eyes, expecting to find the tears that had hovered at the edges of her consciousness ever since the wee hours of the morning, when Ethan had come to her rescue, willing to be a short-term hero, but wary of anything longer than that.

She expected tears. Instead, she slept.

ETHAN FIGURED the meeting would be packed with the PPS staffers who'd agreed to remain in the Vault for as long as it took to bring Clive Fuentes and the TCM conspirators to justice. Instead, he found Evangeline sitting alone in the conference room with her face in her hands.

He paused for a moment before crossing to her and touching her shoulder. "Hey. Need someone to lean on? That seems to be my specialty this week."

She unfolded to look at him, and a faintly wistful expression crossed her face before she shook her head. "Thanks, but it's not your problem, and I don't think either of us really wants it to become your problem. Things are complicated enough as it is."

"True." They'd never really talked about the hint of attraction that had laced their friendship since the very beginning.

He'd been at the lowest of the low, six months after Caro's death, when he'd met Evangeline through a mutual acquaintance and she'd offered him a job. After he'd turned her down three or four times, she'd offered him a freelance assignment instead. When he'd completed the protection detail, she'd given him another. And another. By the time he realized he'd become one of the lost souls she was determined to save, it was too late for resentment. He and Evangeline had formed the sort of bond that developed between the survivors of horrible tragedies, though he'd told her only part of his story.

It was more than he'd told anyone else, and he valued the friendship, so he gave her hands a squeeze and dropped into the chair beside her. "So how is your day going?"

She blew out a breath on a half laugh. "Crappy. Really, really crappy. Robert's in Spain, where the others think they have a bead on Clive. When he called to say he'd landed safely, Angel dumped the call and forgot to give me the message." She shot him a sidelong glance. "Let's just say I owe her an apology for my reaction when I found out."

Ethan shrugged. "She seemed fine when I asked her to rustle up a computer and phone for Nicole." Which brought his thoughts circling back around to a soft-haired, violet-eyed place they had no business being. He cleared his throat. "Any word from the team in Madrid?"

"Robert is supposed to rendezvous with them first thing in the morning. John is positive Clive is holed up in a little village up the coast. That's the good news. The bad news is that they don't have anything new connecting him to TCM, the murders or the oil scheme."

Ethan blew out a breath. "Which means we're still not even sure how many shadows we're actually chasing."

"It'd help if we knew what Nicole saw up in that elevator. From the speed of the hospital attack, I have to believe she saw something important, something that could lead us to the answers we need."

"I know." The needs of the investigation pushed against Ethan's desire to protect Nicole, not just from her attackers, but from the memories her mind had locked away. Climbing down the side of the building to rescue her had been bad enough, and he'd had belay ropes firmly attached and a couple of beefy firefighters spotting his climb. She'd had nothing but a cracking pane of reinforced glass between her and thin air.

"If she saw something that could help us ID who-ever attacked the offices, she'd be saving lives," Evangeline reminded him.

Ethan nodded. "I'll talk to Dr. Eballa and

see what she suggests. Hypnosis, maybe, or sodium Pentothal. No," he corrected himself, "not Pentothal. No drugs with the, um, with the pregnancy."

When that earned him a sharp look from Evangeline, he grimaced. "We barely know each other. I picked her up at a bar, we got a room and now she's pregnant. Logically, that's not the basis for a lasting relationship." He stood and began to pace, talking as much to himself as to her now. "Caro and I planned on having kids, but that was different. We'd chosen each other first and the baby was going to come after, once we were absolutely sure we were ready. Then—" When grief and guilt balled hot in his chest, he broke off, already regretting his uncharacteristic outburst. "Sorry. Not your problem."

Evangeline tilted her head. "It might not be a problem if you gave her a chance."

Because he was almost tempted, Ethan's answer came out harsher than he'd intended. "No. I don't want the baby, and I don't want her."

At that, he heard a small sound from the doorway.

Gut fisting on a surge of guilt, he turned to see Nicole standing just inside the room, her hand still on the doorknob. Her eyes were wide and dark in her pale face.

Damning himself, Ethan took a step toward her. "I didn't know you were there. I'm—"

"Don't," she said, lifting a hand to cut him off. "You've been honest—if not quite that blunt—with me already. You don't want to be a father. I get it. I'm not here because I'm trying to change your mind, I'm here because someone's trying to kill me." She jammed her hands into the pockets of her ragged jeans, and continued. "No offense, but the accommodations aren't exactly cushy, so I think we should do whatever it takes to figure out what I saw the other day." She looked from Ethan to Evangeline and back. "So what's the plan, hypnosis?"

Evangeline nodded. "That's one possibility."

"Let's do it. The sooner I get my memory back, the sooner I can get on with my life." She spun on her heel, then paused and glanced back. "In the interim, I'm going to need to borrow some clothes. Preferably not Angel's."

Then she was gone, the door shutting firmly in her wake.

Ethan stared after her for a long moment before he blew out a breath. "Well. That was bad timing."

But though he regretted hurting her, it wasn't fair to let her think they had a future together.

THE FOLLOWING DAY, the clock on Nic's borrowed laptop said it was close to lunchtime when Angel came for her.

"This way." The receptionist led Nic past the conference rooms and back out to the garage, where Evangeline waited in a sleek black BMW.

"We're leaving the Vault?" A spurt of unease dampened Nic's pleasure at the thought of non-recycled air.

"We can't compromise the security of the Vault by bringing in outsiders." One corner of her mouth kicked up. "Besides, those jeans are all I have to loan you. Even with the drive time, we've got an hour to spare before the hypnotist and sketch artist are meeting us at the station. I thought we could find ourselves a mall."

Nic's heart lifted fleetingly at the thought

of doing something normal like hitting a department store. "You're on."

Thirty minutes and a couple of hundred dollars later, Nic paid for her purchases in cash Evangeline had taken from an emergency stash. But although she had a badly needed change of clothes, Nic was far edgier than she'd been back at the Vault.

Evangeline constantly surveyed their surroundings with a professional's eye, which made Nic stare at the passersby, wondering if one of them wanted her dead. In addition, there was Ethan. Neither woman mentioned his name, but he lingered just beyond their desultory conversation, bringing an added tension that had a vicious headache prickling behind Nic's eyeballs by the time they returned to the BMW and loaded their bags in the trunk.

Once they were back on the road, Evangeline popped the center console and dug out a distinctive red-and-white bottle. "You want a Tylenol? I brought some along."

"Thanks." Nic downed a tablet. "That was thoughtful of you."

"They were in case my arm started bugging me." Evangeline flexed halfway, stopping with a wince. Then she sent Nic a sidelong glance. "And Ethan asked me to look out for you."

Instead of asking what he'd said, or where he'd been since the day before, Nic stared out the passenger-side window, seeing nothing. "How much further to the station?"

"We're almost there." Evangeline paused. "Listen, I'm the last person who should be giving relationship advice, but I know Ethan so I'm going to say it anyway. Don't give up on him yet."

Nic snorted. "There's nothing to give up."

"There could be." Evangeline's face was stern in profile as she drove, and faintly haggard with lack of sleep. "Look, when I met him, he was in a really bad place. Something bad happened, and he felt responsible. Heck, he still does, and I think he's using it as an excuse to be a loner."

Nic glanced over. "Why are you telling me this?"

"Because I want him to be happy, and right now I don't think he knows what's going to make him happy." Before Nic could respond, Evangeline turned into a parking garage, took the first available spot and announced,

"We're here. Come on. They'll be waiting for us."

She was out of the car like a shot, leaving Nic to wonder whether there'd been an ulterior motive to the other woman's advice.

Inside the police station, Detective Riske met them just inside the door, her sharp face tensing when she saw Evangeline. "Mr. Moore called me when he couldn't get through on your cell."

Evangeline blanched. "I forgot to turn it back on after two days of landlines. What's wrong? Is it Robert?"

"I'm sorry," the detective said, eyes darkening with regret. "Apparently there was a skirmish south of Madrid."

"Is he dead?"

"They're not sure. He's disappeared."

Chapter Seven

Spain

"Let me out of here, you bastard!" For what seemed like the hundredth time, Robert lifted his bound legs and slammed them against the metal wall beside him. The echo boomed on the dry, hot air, but there was no sound from outside the metal container where he was being held.

The dimensions of the space, along with a pair of small vents and a locked rolling door at one end suggested he'd been tossed in the back of a box truck. The vehicle hadn't moved in the hour or so since he'd regained consciousness, indicating that they'd parked him.

But where?

"Bugger it," he muttered, cursing himself as much as them.

One minute he'd been huddling with a handful of PPS's most experienced operatives, fine-tuning the plan to grab Clive when he returned to the small house he'd rented south of Madrid. In the next minute, all hell had broken loose. He remembered a blur of knife-wielding locals and the pop of handgun fire, and nothing after that.

His arm hurt like hell, but as best he could tell in the dim, filtered light, the wound had bled freely and scabbed over, leaving him smelling of blood and sweat. "No tears, though," he said aloud, dry lips cracking when he smiled at his own joke.

The thought of tears had him remembering the scene at the airport, tingeing his desperate situation with an added layer of grief.

He should've handled Evangeline better. He should've handled a lot of things better since his return from Cuerva, but he'd found his social skills rusty, his skills as a husband even worse. He'd spent two years with her image firmly in his mind, but on some level he'd forgotten how strong-willed she could be, how independent. He'd expected a reunion and gotten resentment instead, and that had triggered his own stubborn streak, leaving them at odds when they should've been working together. And now…

Now she was back in the States, once again receiving word that he was missing, maybe even presumed dead.

At the thought of it, at the image of her perfect face stained with tears and grief, he did the only thing he could think to do.

He lifted his bound legs and slammed them into the metal wall again, hoping against hope that someone would hear.

Colorado, USA

"DOES THIS look like what you saw?" The sketch artist spun her laptop and showed Nic the image on the screen.

Nic frowned at the silhouette image of a helicopter, concentrating on the scattershot mental images the hypnotist had managed to retrieve. She'd regained her memory of most of the elevator ride, right up to the actual moment of impact. She also remembered those terrifying minutes after she'd regained consciousness, when Ethan had been climbing down to rescue her, and she'd been sure she would fall to her death at any moment. Oddly enough, those images seemed somehow cushioned, with a misty gray curtain distancing her from immediate terror. She suspected she had the hypnotist— a tall, thin man with a pronounced right hook to his nose—to thank for that.

Unfortunately, her memories of the helicopter's inhabitants remained fuzzy. She'd been able to remember only that there had been a pilot and one passenger sitting beside him, along with a tall man with a rocket launcher who might or might not have been the guy who'd been in her hospital room. Luckily, though, she was clearer on the machine itself. In theory, if she could help identify the make and model, the investigators should be able to track down its registration, or at least narrow the search.

She squinted at the photo, comparing it to the newly-remembered images in her brain. "The helicopter's nose was longer and more streamlined, and I think the thing on the tail was taller."

The sketch artist, an energetic, bespectacled woman in her mid-fifties who'd proved to be more of a computer modeler than a pen-and-paper artist, nodded and spun the laptop back around to face her. Two iterations later, they had their helicopter.

After a quick database search, the artist said, "It's probably military surplus, maybe an MI-2 or -8. They have a range of five hundred miles or so, a top speed of about a hundred-fifty. They're not rare in civilian use, but it's less of a needle in a haystack than it was."

Detective Riske rose to her feet. "I'm on it." She offered Nicole her hand. "Thank you. We appreciate you coming in, and submitting to hypnosis. I can't imagine it was pleasant."

"Better that than doing nothing while someone else dies," Nic said quietly. While waiting for the artist, she'd learned that a young girl had been killed by debris that had fallen from the office building after the attack. The child and her mother had been minding their own business on the street when death had fallen from the sky.

How quickly life could change, Nic thought as she rose and collected her new lightweight jacket and a half-full bottle of soda. The point was brought home moments later when she passed the front desk and saw who was waiting to drive her back to the Vault.

It was Ethan.

SHE WAS PALE, he saw, even beneath an added hint of makeup. The new clothes flattered her with a practical, no-nonsense style he couldn't help admiring.

He'd managed to stay away from her for almost twenty-four hours, but it had seemed like longer, and when she passed him on her way to the exit and he caught her subtle, flowery scent, it was all he could do to keep himself from closing his eyes and inhaling.

"How bad was the hypnosis?" he asked as he escorted her to the Jeep and held the passenger's door for her.

"I survived," she said, her expression giving away nothing. "Detective Riske is going to look for a military surplus helicopter, maybe something called an MI-8. Black, with no FAA numbers."

"I'll look into it," he said as he swung into the driver's side and fired up the engine. "PPS has access to a few more databases than the cops."

She glanced over at him. "Has there been any word on Robert?"

He hit the gas a little too hard, shooting them out of the parking garage and onto the streets beyond. "It was an ambush. A setup. Somehow Clive knew we were onto him and used himself as bait. When the team moved in, they walked straight into a trap." He blew out a breath, gut grinding at the frustration of not being there, of not being able to help.

For the first time in a long, long time, he regretted having kept himself at the edge of things. He was one of the PPS operatives yet not one of them, a member of the team while still being a man apart.

Nic frowned at a passing street sign. "You're headed away from the Vault. Are you afraid we're being followed?"

"I always assume I'm being followed. That's what makes me a good bodyguard." Or it usually did. Now, though, he was distracted and not at top form. "But we're not going straight back to the Vault. There's someone I'd like you to meet, first." Ethan's fingers tightened on the steering wheel until he could feel the imprint of the plastic in his flesh at the thought of Blake Rothschild, a former protectee who owed him a favor.

Blake was loaded with family money so old it smelled musty, and cheerfully donated time and cash to everything from Save the Spotted Newt to an inventor who was halfway to building an antigravity unit. Blake was also charming, handsome, personable, fiercely loyal…

And he wanted a family.

NIC STAYED silent as Ethan drove them south out of Denver to Sedalia, an upscale area very near the legendary Denver Polo Club. She knew the area because Jonah used to drive her through it, boasting that they'd live there once he'd landed a few more big clients. Or had gotten a promotion. Or been made partner. The ambition seemed to expand each time they went on one of their "tours," with the promises getting wilder, the houses getting bigger and grander.

Though none so grand as the one Ethan turned toward, winding up a long, tree-lined driveway that led to a mansion.

The circular drive was paved with cement bricks in interspersed patterns of red, gray and tan that arched around a central planting bed where three old trees shaded a small fountain. The house itself blended the best of modern and classical architecture, with huge, airy windows, wrought-iron balustrades and strategic touches of brick. Wide granite steps led up to the front entrance, which was flanked with upright columns of local stone that had been turned into art by the wearing effects of wind and rain.

Instead of leading her up to the heavy front door, with its inset stained glass, Ethan gestured her around the side of the house, along a more modest brick walkway flanked with seasonal plantings and colored gravel.

"Servant's entrance?" she quipped when they reached a normal-looking door.

"Nah," he answered. "Friends, neighbors and people not looking for donations." He pushed open the door partway and called, "Yo, Blake!"

Footsteps sounded moments later and the door swung open to reveal a tall, lean man in his late thirties, with shaggy light brown hair, kind mid-blue eyes and a faintly crooked nose. In a crisp white button-down shirt, untucked and with the sleeves rolled up on his tanned forearms, along with comfortably tailored navy pants and a pair of quillwork moccasins, he was probably wearing a thousand dollars worth of clothes on a casual stay-at-home day. Framed in the brick-faced doorway, with glimpses of polished wood and oriental carpets visible behind him, he should have looked unapproachable, like something out of the glossy magazines Nic flipped through in line at the grocery store.

Instead, when he smiled and held out a hand, she felt as if she'd known him forever.

"It's a pleasure to meet you, Nicole. I'm Blake Rothschild." His handshake was firm but undemanding, and he moved with innate grace when he stepped back and ushered them inside. "Please."

This, Nic realized as she stepped inside a home that she immediately saw *was* a home, despite its size and grandeur, this was what Jonah-the-jerk had always wanted to be and never quite managed to pull off. Blake Rothschild, however, managed it in spades. That very fact—and the parallel between the two men—should have put her on alert. Instead, she felt the tickle of warmth that came from meeting someone she immediately knew she could be friends with.

"This way." He led them down a short hallway that was mostly windows on one side, with the opposite wall painted a pale mint-green and hung with a series of water-colors depicting local scenes, both the city and the mountains beyond.

Ethan nodded to the paintings. "Blake's work."

"They're lovely," Nicole said, and she meant it, but that didn't explain the connection between the two men, or why Ethan had brought her here. When Blake paused at a doorway and gestured for her to precede him through, she paused and looked up at him. "You're a painter?"

His lips quirked. "Ethan didn't tell you why he wanted us to meet, did he?"

Nicole was reassured by the easy friendship between the men, but nerves danced across her skin and gathered in her belly as she crossed a cozy yet masculine library, and a new suspicion began to take shape. What if Ethan had decided to clear his conscience by finding their baby a substitute father? Her suspicion only intensified when Blake gestured her to a mahogany-legged leather sofa and took the matching chair opposite her, but Ethan remained standing near the door.

Blake caught her quick look in that direction. "He's very good. But then, we both know that, don't we?"

Nicole frowned. "Excuse me?"

"Ethan spent a short stint here about a year ago, guarding me." Blake pantomimed a shooting motion in Ethan's direction, then answered her question, saying, "The painting is a hobby. In real life, I run a telecommunications R & D boutique, very high-tech, very specialized. I was competing with several other companies for the rights to a nanochip patent, and began receiving some, shall we say, less than complimentary communications from an overseas competitor."

In other words, he'd gotten death threats, Nic realized. "Ethan was your bodyguard?"

"Exactly. I offered him a permanent position, but you know Ethan. He's not the settling-down type."

As if punctuating the point, Ethan's cell phone rang. He flipped it open and checked the display, and his expression blanked. He looked from Nic to Blake and back. "I need to take this. Will you two be okay?"

"We're fine." Blake waved him off. "I reset the alarm once we were inside, and the perimeter motion detectors are on. Nobody's getting to her in here."

Ethan sent Nic a long, unreadable look before he answered the call on the fourth ring as he headed through the door, his voice and footsteps receding down the hallway.

"Ethan told me about your situation," Blake said without preamble. "I know how stressed out you must be. I think I can help."

Almost positive Ethan had planned this as a setup, as a way to assuage his guilt over what she'd overheard the other day, Nic said, "You don't strike me as the type to date unwed single mothers-to-be."

There was a long moment of silence before Blake coughed, and then grinned. "Ethan didn't tell me about that part. He said you'd witnessed an attack and now you have people gunning for you. I remember how awful it was to not be able to step outside my door without armed protection."

"Oh." Nic's face flamed and her stomach knotted in enormous embarrassment. She'd just made an assumption based on almost no data. "Oh, jeez, I'm sorry. I thought…" She trailed off and waited for a second, hoping the floor would open up and swallow her, so she wouldn't have to face a man—a very rich, successful man—she'd all but accused of wanting…what? An instant family? "I don't know what I was thinking. Can we chalk it up to temporary insanity brought on by hormones?"

He laughed. "Consider it done, and we'll get down to business."

"What business?"

"Ethan also told me you're in need of an investor for biofuel R & D, and he knows that I'm always looking to underwrite small inventors, particularly when they're connected to education." While Nic gaped at him, he leaned back and folded his hands behind his head. "Go ahead. Hit me with your best pitch. Tell me why I should fund your project."

Chapter Eight

Spain

As she spoke into the landline phone, Evangeline kept her back to the wall and her attention on the passing airport travelers. She pitched her voice to carry over the background hum of mixed languages, Spanish predominating. "I'll call you once I hook up with the others and we've pulled together a plan."

Ethan's voice was subdued when he said, "I wish you'd talked to me about this before you left."

"Why, so you could tell me not to go?" She blew out a frustrated breath as part of her wished she hadn't called him. Angel knew she'd left the Vault, and the team in Madrid knew she was on her way... but she'd wanted—needed—somebody to worry about her as a person. Under other circumstances, that would've been Robert. Given the present situation, Ethan had gotten the call. Now she said, "Think of it this way, I saved you the argument." When he didn't reply, she lowered her voice and went with the truth. "Look, I know you don't approve, and you've probably got a point, but I can't—I *won't*—sit around back home and wait while other people look for my husband. Not ever again."

"I know. Just be careful, will you? PPS can't lose you. And just think of how Robert would feel if they get him out and something's happened to you."

Nearby, a heavyset man was wearing dark sunglasses that seemed out of place against the gray day outside the Madrid Barajas International Airport. Evangeline narrowed her eyes and watched him as she said, "I thought you didn't like Robert."

"I'm warming to him."

Evangeline snorted, partly from amusement, partly from relief that Señor Sunglasses had walked right past her to cheek-kiss an older woman schlepping two rolling suitcases. "I'll be careful, I promise. If you don't believe me, call one of the guys and check up on me."

"I'll do that," he said, but they both knew he wouldn't. Though he'd been working at PPS for over a year, he didn't consider himself one of the team. In his mind, he was still an independent contractor working on the fringes.

"Take care of things back at the Vault for me, okay?" she said softly, suddenly nervous that she might never see home again.

"Of course. I'll e-mail updates to your account as warranted, since Cam said the Internet is more reliable than the international phone connections over there." He paused, and she heard voices in the background. "Take care of yourself. I mean it."

"You, too," she said, and cut the connection before she said anything else, anything that might stray too close to the strange line she and Ethan had walked for the past eighteen months, a gray area of more than friendship, less than something else. She'd seen him mourn his wife, Caro. He'd sat with her as she'd wept for Robert, a luxury she hadn't allowed herself in front of anyone else. They'd leaned on each other. They liked each other. And they both knew it was time to change things. At least she did.

Sometimes, she wondered whether Ethan intended to keep running forever, and whether he was going to run right past something wonderful.

Shaking her head, she reached down and grabbed the lightweight carry-on duffel that held everything she figured she'd need in Spain: two changes of wash-and-wear clothing, the basic makeup she considered necessary for a put-together woman in her forties, her laptop and her diary, which went wherever she did. She didn't necessarily write in it every day—sometimes she went for months without adding a line, but her childhood in the foster system had taught her that history was precious.

As she shouldered the duffel, she thought about adding an entry for the first time in a long while. Maybe later tonight, after she'd connected with the guys and they'd brought her up to speed on the search for Robert. Or maybe, just maybe, they'd already found him. Maybe he'd be waiting for her, ticked off because she'd left the safety of the Vault, but a little bit glad to see her, all the same.

Holding the image of his reluctant, sharp-edged smile at the forefront of her mind, she headed for the taxi queue. She was halfway there when someone bumped her from behind and she stumbled forward.

A strong hand caught her arm and kept her from falling, and a man's voice said, *"Perdone!"*

"No problem," she said, and stepped away so he'd release his grip. He tightened it, instead. That was when she focused on his face and her guts went to water.

"Actually, there *is* a problem," Clive Fuentes said in accentless English. The handsome Spaniard was six feet tall and in his mid-sixties, with dark hair and near-black eyes almost obscured behind tinted lenses. He wore a lightweight navy suit, white shirt, tie and shined shoes, allowing him to blend immaculately with the business commuters in the busy baggage claim area.

She'd bet most of those commuters weren't carrying pistols in their pockets, though. She could feel the press of it just above her hip as he held her arm in one hand, the concealed weapon in the other.

"I won't bother with the dramatic threats,"

he said conversationally. "We're both professionals, and you know exactly what I'm capable of. Which is why you're going to smile, and we're going to walk out of here, nice and easy. Any questions?"

Heart lodged in her throat, Evangeline shook her head slowly, trying to keep her hands and legs from trembling as Clive hustled her out of the airport and shoved her into a waiting limousine.

Colorado, USA

ON THEIR WAY back to the Vault, Ethan spent most of the ride on his cell phone. Nic knew darned well he was avoiding talking to her about Blake, who had offered flat-out to fund the biofuel project.

Thanks to Ethan, she had her funding. She should've been celebrating, should've wanted to thank him. Instead, she wanted to strangle him, because if she'd suspected earlier that the visit to Blake's house had been a setup, Ethan's passing comment about Sedalia being a great place to raise a family had sealed it.

Blake might not know it yet, but Ethan

was trying to pass her off on a friend. A rich, handsome friend, granted, but still.

"No," he snapped into the phone. "I don't want to talk to him. You two are just going to have to work it out yourselves."

As far as Nic could tell, he was trying to mediate an argument between two of the computer techs back at the Vault, and not doing a very good job of it. Annoyed with the whole lot of them, she said, "Give me the phone."

Ethan was so startled by her tone—or fed up with the techies—he handed it over.

"This is Nicole Benedict," she said into the phone. "What do you want on your pizza?"

There was dead silence. Then a voice said, "Huh?"

Moments later, a second voice said, "Pineapple."

The first voice immediately shouted, "No pineapple. I hate pineapple."

"Quiet!" Nic barked. "Make a list. There're what, twenty of you splitting shifts? So figure eight or ten pizzas, along with salads and soda. Text the list to this phone." She hung up without waiting for an answer, and passed the phone back to Ethan. "Find us a pizza joint."

He kept his attention on the road, but after a moment, the corner of his mouth kicked up. "It wasn't about the fight, was it?"

Nic shook her head. "Their office was blown up with most of them inside it, they were hustled out to the middle of nowhere, and now they're cooped up together, breathing down each other's necks and not making much progress. Evangeline was doing her best to keep it level in there. With her gone, something was bound to set them off. Doesn't matter who or what the fight was about, it's a symptom of a different problem."

"And pizza's the cure?"

"Think of it as a pepperoni Band-Aid," she suggested. "And be aware that you're going to have to do your share of mediating once we're back inside. You might want to make them run the halls or something, given that there's no gym. There's a reason NASA spends a good chunk of its budget on psych testing: human beings don't do so well cooped up together for extended periods."

"Great." Ethan pinched the bridge of his nose as though warding off a headache. "This is so not what I need right now."

"Well, it's what you've got, so deal," Nic said.

He glanced over at her. "I don't suppose you'd care to play den mother?"

"I'll help," she said, "but you're not dumping it all on me. It won't kill you to get to know a few of your coworkers."

He grimaced, but took the next left. "I'm pretty sure there's a mom-and-pop pizzeria down here a mile or so."

They drove in silence for a minute before guilt prickled and Nic said, "I take it back. I'll do the den-mother thing. You focus on your work."

He slid her a look. "That was quick."

She lifted a shoulder. "I owe you for introducing me to Blake."

When the corners of his mouth went tight, she couldn't help feeling a small spurt of satisfaction. Then the phone beeped to announce the arrival of the texted food order, and they spent the next few minutes finding a pizza joint and convincing the teenage girl behind the counter to put a rush on the order.

Less than a half hour later they were back on the road, with Ethan doubling back to check for pursuit before heading the Jeep toward the Vault. They were nearly there when a new text message came in. It said simply: chpper fnd, reg to TCM.

"Hot damn." Ethan stepped on the accelerator, edging the speedometer toward seventy-five mph. "Amazing what a little bribery will do."

Ethan and Nic navigated the three-layer security, parked the Jeep and entered the Vault. When they reached the mess hall, the staffers descended on the pizza boxes en masse. They immediately started wrangling over who'd ordered what, but Nic figured the friendly bickering was an improvement.

A woman around Nic's own age crossed to Ethan and handed him a thin folder. "An MI-8 military surplus helicopter used to be registered to the west-coast branch of TCM. About three months ago, they replaced it with a custom-built Augusta 109 Executive helicopter. The MI-8 was taken off the books and resold to one of those helicopter tour places."

Ethan frowned. "So it's not connected to TCM anymore?"

"That's where it gets interesting." She retrieved the folder, flipped it open and pointed to several entries in a data spreadsheet. "The chopper tour company, Rocky Mountain Sky, is real enough. It'd have to be in order to pass FAA scrutiny these days. Thing is, look at what they're flying, and how often."

Nic peered over Ethan's shoulder as he tapped the spreadsheet and said, "Rocky Mountain Sky has two other helicopters, both smaller birds that are a lot cheaper to run than the MI-8."

"How do you know that?" she asked.

"I wanted to fly choppers when I was in the service, but got sent for medic training instead," he said shortly, then continued, "It's certainly possible that they decided to upgrade, but look at this." He indicated another line in the flight log. "The MI-8 hasn't been flown from their heliport in a couple of weeks. What do you want to bet it's not at Rocky Mountain Sky anymore?"

The female staffer nodded. "One of our people on the outside is checking into it, and we're looking to see who actually owns the tour company. If we can connect it back to someone at TCM and prove that the bird isn't where it's supposed to be, we might have enough to take to the cops."

"It's tenuous, but it could work." He nodded to the woman. "Good job. Get yourself some pizza before it's all gone."

When she had departed, Nic said, "This doesn't help you figure out how Clive Fuentes is involved, though, does it?"

"No, but there's usually more than one way to work a case. If I come at it from this angle while the team in Spain works on finding Robert and capturing Clive, we should be able to close the net."

"Have you heard from Evangeline?"

"I talked to her just after she landed. She'll call when she meets up with the team and they've got a plan in place. When she does, I'd like to have this helicopter thing nailed down."

Nic nodded. "Why don't I grab some pizza for both of us and meet you in the main computer room?"

"I'll take the food, but you don't have to stay," he said as he turned away. "You should get some rest."

She touched his shoulder, stopping him. When he turned back, she said, "It's my fight now, too, Ethan."

He shook his head. "Thanks for the offer,

but I'm the professional here. We need to play to our strengths."

Which was part of the problem, Nic realized with a rush of frustration. Some days she felt like she'd walked away from her strengths years earlier, when Jonah-the-jerk had urged her to quit grad school and she'd given in.

Refusing to back down again, she lifted her chin and shot Ethan a defiant look. "I have three years of grad school and a biofuel project that says research *is* one of my strengths. So give me a thread to pull and I'll do my best with it. What have you got to lose?"

He shot her a dark look, but shuffled a page out of the folder. "Okay, Sherlock. Here's the call number of the ownership transfer for that chopper. I want to know who at TCM signed off on the sale."

THEY WORKED side by side as one hour slipped into the next. There were no windows, but Ethan could feel the sunset in his bones, the product of many hours and days spent hiking in the wilderness, alone with nothing but his own thoughts for company, just the way he liked it.

Surprisingly, he found he didn't mind

working near Nicole nearly as much as he'd feared. He was aware of her, but the distraction was more physical than mental, so he forced himself to focus on the computer trails and phone chains rather than the hint of her subtle scent on the air currents within the underground room.

Everything took him twice as long as it would have taken Cam or John, making him wish he'd taken Evangeline up on her offer of training him as an investigator, not just a bodyguard.

Down the hall, the pizza party continued unabated, the happy sounds a necessary break from the stress of the past few days. It'd been a close call, but he'd handled it, making him think he could handle the rest. He could keep the sequestered PPS staff on track while the team in Madrid found Robert and captured Clive, and he could keep his hands off Nicole while they found the last few pieces necessary to topple the stick house TCM had assembled of investors and shell companies.

And when that was done, they could all go back to their lives. He could go back to the short-term assignments he loved best, and

Nicole could return to her classes on schedule, armed with Blake's help for the biofuel project.

And if the thought of them together made Ethan grind his teeth hard enough that his jaw cracked, he'd just have to deal.

"Found it!" Nicole said suddenly. She pushed away from the computer station, eyes gleaming with satisfaction. "The TCM helicopter sale was authorized by a woman named Olivia Turner."

"Really?" Ethan blinked, trying to realign his thoughts. "Huh!"

"I take it she's not a prime suspect?"

"Not even close." He frowned, trying to recall everything he knew about a woman who'd only really nicked the edges of their investigation. "She was Robert's first wife, which would seem like a valid connection on the surface, but now she's married to Stephen Turner, the head of TCM. He's been cleared of all suspicion. Heck, he's helping fund the PPS investigation in an effort to figure out who was using TCM resources to profit from the oil-rights pyramid and the murders. Besides, Olivia and Robert's son, Kyle, is Stephen's second-in-command, and he's a stand-up guy. They're both clean as far as we know."

"You're talking about Stephen and Kyle, not Olivia," Nic pointed out. "Don't tell me you're discounting Olivia because she's a woman?"

"No," he countered. "I'm discounting her because she's…" He trailed off, trying to find a way to de-scribe Turner's wife. "She's not all there. Rumor has it she was a little off before all this started, but a couple of months ago her other son, Peter, was shot by the cops and put in a coma. Since then, she's been sliding hard."

Nicole pursed her lips. "A sane person wouldn't shoot a rocket into an office building."

"True, but the conspiracy has been planned far too precisely for her to be directly involved," Ethan argued, then paused when another thought occurred to him. "However, Peter was one of the main cogs. I'll bet he either talked his mother into okaying the helicopter sale, or flat-out forged her signature."

Which meant they'd just tied the helicopter lead to a conspirator who was already out of the picture.

"Darn it," Nicole muttered, apparently

reaching the same conclusion. "Well, maybe we'll be able to connect Rocky Mountain Sky to someone else."

"Fingers crossed." Ethan turned back to his machine and checked his e-mail on the off chance one of his contacts had already caught his query.

"What else can I help with?"

"Give me a minute." Sure enough, he'd gotten a hit on his request for incorporation papers for the tour company, thanks to a PPS contact named Scoot. "I may be onto something."

"I'll go grab more sodas." She stood and collected the remains of their dinner. "Be back in five."

He didn't respond as he bent to his work.

Nic was halfway down the hall when the lights went out.

She gasped, more from surprise than fear, and her low cry was echoed farther along the hall, where the others were gathered. Frozen in her tracks, she thought, *It's probably nothing, just a glitch.*

Moments later, emergency lights kicked on overhead, lighting the darkness.

Relieved, Nic hurried to the galley-style kitchen, where the others had gone quiet. "Is everyone okay in here?"

"What's going on?" demanded a computer tech named Zach. In his mid-forties, he was among the oldest of the bunch, but looked the closest to panic. "What was that noise?"

Nic shook her head. "I didn't hear any noise."

A split second later, a dull thudding surrounded them. Almost below the level of hearing, the vibration transmitted through the floor to the soles of her feet.

"That noise!" Zach said, eyes wild. "We heard it right before the lights went out. Is someone bombing us?"

"We're in a bomb shelter," another voice said. To Nic's surprise, Angel pushed through the shifting bodies and joined her at the front of the crowd. "This is the safest place to be if something bad is happening outside."

Nic thought fleetingly that they were in pretty serious trouble if Angel was making sense.

There was a clatter out in the hallway, and Ethan skidded into the room with a small, snub-nosed pistol in one hand, a penlight in the other. His eyes went immediately to Nic, and he stopped in his tracks and exhaled a long breath. "You're okay."

"We all are," she confirmed, refusing to feel a sneaky sense of warmth that he'd been worried for her. "Do you have any idea what—"

"Listen!" Zach shouted. "What's *that* noise?"

Nic's first instinct was to tell the guy to get a grip. Then she heard it, too—not a thud, but a hissing noise that brought a faint, strange odor.

Gas!

Moments later, the alarms went off, a whooping din and confusion of flashing lights that was too little, too late. Angel lunged across the room and slapped a panel beside the door, bringing a video monitor to life.

It showed a cluster of gas-masked figures just inside the main door.

Ethan cursed, grabbed Nic and hustled her out of the kitchen, shouting, "Everyone follow me! Stay close and don't touch anything."

They fled through the mazelike halls in a

thunder of footsteps and panicked breathing, headed away from the front entrance. Within minutes, Ethan had turned away from the familiar corridors and plunged down a dark hallway where there were no emergency lights.

"Where are we going?" Nic kept her voice low, so the others wouldn't hear.

Ethan did the same when he answered, "Evangeline showed me the original blueprints of this installation. There should be—" He broke off and made a low sound of satisfaction when his small flashlight beam shone on a door marked Emergency Supplies.

Finding the door locked, he gestured for the others to stand back. "Give me some room. I'm going to try to control the ricochet, but you never know."

Nic huddled with the others in a miserable, scared knot.

"I smell something," Zach whispered.

She would have snapped at him to shut the heck up, but she smelled it, too, a faintly rotten odor that crinkled the hairs inside her nose and made her want to cough.

Hurry, Ethan, she thought. *Hurry!*

He blasted the lock and kicked the door

open, then disappeared into the room, his path lit only by the faint luminance of his penlight. Moments later, the light brightened considerably and he reappeared carrying a half-dozen larger, military-type flashlights. He shook his head. "No gas masks, but take these." He passed out the flashlights.

Nic accepted one and snapped it on. As the scared group followed Ethan down the long, unlit corridor, she pressed her sleeve to her nose and mouth, trying to filter out the gas. Still, her head spun and her feet dragged against each other as Ethan turned down another hallway.

Behind her, she heard someone fall, heard the others dragging the fallen person up and onward. Instead of panicking, Nic sped up to match Ethan's pace and touched his hand. When he looked over at her, she said, "You can do this." She halfway expected him to push her away, to push away the responsibility he'd been saddled with.

Instead, he took her hand and squeezed it, and led her into the darkness.

Chapter Nine

Spain

Robert had been in the sun-baked box truck for nearly two days without food—and more importantly, without water—when he finally heard someone outside. Survival instincts clamored for him to make noise and attract attention, but his MI6 training had him keeping quiet until he figured out whether the approaching footsteps belonged to friend or foe.

He had his answer moments later, when he heard the sounds of a padlock being undone, followed by the rattle of chains and the metallic clanks of the accordion door being unlatched. Feigning unconsciousness, he lay limply on his side with his arms and legs still bound and his face pressed against the dirty floor of the box compartment. He positioned himself to face the door, though, and kept his eyelids slitted.

It was all he could do to keep himself still when the door rolled up to reveal a heavyset, bearded stranger holding an unconscious Evangeline draped over his shoulder, fireman-style.

Rage roared through Robert, tensing his limbs and bringing his heartbeat to a thunder in his ears at the sight of her, bruised and battered and unutterably beautiful.

And captured, goddamn it.

Behind her captor, Clive Fuentes gestured with a pistol. "Toss her in. I'd rather kill them and dump the bodies, but they still have value to me for another day." He looked directly at Robert. "You hear that, Robert? You've got twenty-four hours to say goodbye to your wife."

His age-graveled voice still held the tones of years earlier, when he'd been Robert's friend and mentor.

The betrayal banded Robert's muscles like iron, making them tremble with hatred. Clive had tried to kill him, all but ruining his marriage in the process. And for what? Oil revenue and a dirty investment scheme. What a waste of an agent, of a human being who'd once done the right thing.

Robert forced himself to stay still as the bearded thug unceremoniously dumped Evangeline near the door. The guy shot Clive a look. "You want to tie her or anything?"

Clive scowled. "What's the worst she can do in the next twenty-four, pull his zip ties off? That won't get them out of the truck, and it won't change the fact that we're practically in the middle of nowhere." He waved to the door. "Just lock 'em in. Won't matter if they make noise. Heck, none of it is going to matter after tomorrow."

With that, he reached up and yanked on a dangling strap. The accordion door rolled down and closed with a decisive slam, followed by the clank and clatter of the padlock.

Robert opened his eyes the same moment Evangeline opened hers. In the weak daylight that filtered through vents high overhead, they locked gazes, not daring to speak yet, not daring to move. He drank in the sight of her, and the relief that her eyes were clear and angry, good evidence that she'd been faking unconsciousness as thoroughly as he had.

Are you okay? he mouthed, fearing the dark bruise on the porcelain skin of her cheek might indicate worse injuries elsewhere.

But her lips quirked, then shaped the words, *I'm okay. You?*

Fine. But on the heels of relief came sick anger, partly self-directed, partly aimed at his wife. When the sound of footsteps faded with distance and then went silent, he swung around into the partway-seated position he'd perfected over forty-eight hours of being bound hand and foot, with his shoulders pressed against the wall of the truck, his hands at the small of his back and his legs stuck out in front of him. Then he scowled at his wife. "I thought I told you to stay the hell in the Vault."

There was no doubt in his mind that she'd come after him, and been captured in the process. He knew her too well to believe otherwise.

He expected her to snap back at him, to snarl as they'd been doing at each other too often lately. Instead, she climbed to her feet, wincing once or twice, and crossed to him. Then she bent down and pressed a soft kiss to his lips. "One of these days you'll remember that I work with you, not for you."

Then she stood back and lifted the hem of her bedraggled shirt, which had once been a pale pink button-down. At first, his libido kicked in with some seriously kinky images. Then he got it, and anger turned to shock as she peeled a microscopically thin flap of flesh-toned latex away from the small of her back, revealing a flat, button-like device adhered to her skin beside a small chip with tiny fiber leads.

"You're bugged," he said, feeling like a royal ass. "You planned this. God, I love you."

She smiled, but touched a finger to her lips and mouthed, *Are they listening?*

He shook his head. "Why bother? You heard Clive. He doesn't consider me a threat anymore." Which begged the question of why he'd been kept alive thus far.

What—or *who*—was the bastard waiting for?

"Good," Evangeline said. She pulled both devices free and dropped to a cross-legged sitting position. After fiddling with the flat button for a moment, she set it aside on the floor of the box truck, then cued up the miniature transmitter and fixed one of the fibers along her jawline. "Cameron? Can you hear me?"

Robert closed his eyes, beginning to believe he might be given a second chance— or was it a third or fourth chance at this point?—to right things with the people he cared about the most.

"You have our position?" Evangeline said quietly, then nodded. "See you then." But as she was reaching to kill the connection, her hand stilled. "What?"

Robert heard the horror in her voice and immediately leaned forward, though there was no way he could overhear the fiber transmission, so he was forced to wait until she said, "Got it. Out." She killed the connection with a shaking hand, and turned stricken eyes toward him. "The security system at the Vault transmitted an automated Mayday two hours ago. The main door was breached, and there's been no contact from anyone inside since." A tear welled up. "For all we know, they're already dead."

Colorado, USA

ETHAN JOGGED down the narrow tunnel with the others behind him, hoping to hell he hadn't gotten himself turned around in the mazelike corridors.

The tunnel they were in now was old construction, and the air was damp and faintly musty. If he was remembering the schematics correctly, it should lead them to a concealed exit. If he was wrong, they were in serious trouble.

At the thought, he glanced back at Nicole, who hadn't asked for any of this. She followed close behind him, with the PPS personnel strung out at her back. Each footstep was a reminder of the lives depending on him. If their attackers didn't know about the escape hatch, they'd be able to get out and call for help. If the attackers knew, though, he'd just given them a perfect opportunity for an ambush.

The responsibility weighed on him, reminding him why it was best to remain alone. If nobody was depending on him, he couldn't let anyone down.

In the near distance, his flashlight beam picked out where the tunnel dead-ended at an airlock-type door with an old-fashioned wheeled lock.

Nerves fired in his veins. He stopped at the door and waved the others back. "I'm going to have a look around." He focused on Nicole. "Once I'm through the door I want you to shut and lock it behind me. If everything's okay, I'll knock, three short, three long."

She nodded. "Be careful." Her eyes were huge in her pale face.

Don't rely on me, he wanted to tell her. *I've never been good at coming through for people I care about.* But that would've been admitting that he was coming to care, which wasn't good for either of them.

Still, he couldn't stop himself from leaning down and touching his lips to hers. "See you in a few minutes."

Then he spun the lock, shoved open the heavy door and stepped through.

STILL ABLE to taste his quick kiss on her lips, Nic closed the door behind Ethan. If she were on her own, she would've kept it selfishly cracked, needing to know he could get back to safety if he needed to. But she wasn't alone, so she spun the locking mechanism to seal the door, then waited with her hand pressed to the cold metal panel, listening for his knock. Three short, three long, he'd said. A practical code, no-nonsense, like Ethan himself.

"Do you think they're out there?" Angel asked, her voice too loud, so it carried to the others and then echoed into the darkness beyond their flashlight beams.

"Sh. I need to listen." Nic pressed closer to the door, hoping his signal would come soon. The claustrophobia and the panic had been mostly manageable when they were moving, but now, stuck in the narrow, dead-end tunnel, the fear took root and grew.

What if he didn't knock? She couldn't lead them back the way they'd come, but if she couldn't go forward, what then? What if—

Finally, he knocked—three short, three long. Expelling a breath on a relieved rush, she spun the wheel, pushed open the door and stepped through.

The sun was a warm shock after the tunnel's chill, and the sight of Ethan was an even warmer relief. He nodded to her. "We're clear." He lifted his cell phone before tucking it back in his pocket. "I called Blake. He's going to phone Detective Riske and get us some transportation and an escort."

"Where are we going?" Zach asked, voice cracking with exhaustion and stress. "If they found the Vault, they can find us anywhere."

"I'm sending you to the PPS safe house," Ethan said. "It'll be a tight squeeze to get you all in there, but the security's top-notch, and the cops will help lock the place down."

"We were supposed to be safe in the Vault." Zach scowled. "But they came after us anyway. What makes you think we'll be any better off in the safe house?"

"Because they don't want you," Ethan said, expression shuttered. "They want Nicole, and she and I won't be going with you."

A hitch of fear shimmied through Nic's gut alongside an equal measure of relief. She didn't want to be responsible for anyone else getting hurt, and knew that Ethan was right— the others would be better off without her. But at the same time, there was a feeling of safety in numbers, a buffer between her and Ethan.

"Here's how it's going to work," he said. "We'll wait here with the door open, just in case, until Blake and the cops arrive. They're going to take you to the safe house, where you'll stay until Evangeline or another PPS field agent tells you otherwise, got it?" He waited for the reluctant nods, then said, "Since Nic and I aren't going with you, someone else is going to have to be in charge. Who is it?"

To Nic's surprise the group shuffled for a moment, then turned to the dark-haired goth in their center.

Zach said, "Angel's our girl."

When the others nodded in agreement, the receptionist stood up a little straighter, her shoulders came back, and her chin lifted. A new gleam entered her eyes and she nodded, almost hesitantly. "I can do it." When Ethan didn't say anything right away, she insisted, "I can. I know you and the others think I'm a disaster. Even Evangeline treats me differently, and she's the one who wanted me at PPS in the first place. And I deserved it, I know I did—messing up the phone messages and stuff. But I'm better than that. I can *be* better than that, I know I can." She looked back at the others. "If these guys are willing to trust me, then I'd better step up." This time her nod was decisive. "I can do it."

Ethan reached out and clasped her shoulder briefly. "I believe you." He nodded beyond her, to where a big coach bus was pulling up at the side of the road, flanked by police cruisers. "Time to go." He let his hand fall away. "Be careful."

Angel looked from Ethan to Nic and back, worry evident in her dark-shadowed eyes. "You, too. And keep in touch. I'll do my best to coordinate the investigation from the safe house, even without all of our equipment."

"Thanks, but I have a feeling the investigation won't be going on much longer." Ethan waved them to the bus. "Go on, get out of here."

THE BUS pulled out a few minutes later, leaving Nic and Ethan alone, sheltered in a stand of bushes near the concealed emergency exit. She felt the silence crowding her, pressing her closer to his warm, reassuring bulk as dusk darkened the mountainous horizon. "What didn't you want the others to know?" she asked quietly.

He glanced down at her. After a moment's

pause, he said, "I think something went wrong in Madrid. Evangeline's phone went straight to voice mail, which means she turned it off, and she never turns off her phone. I got through to Cam, but he was in a hurry. Wouldn't give me any details, just told me to watch my back. He sounded worried, though, and Cam never worries."

She reached out and gripped his forearm, and felt the tension humming through him. He was afraid for his friends—for Evangeline and the other agents, for Angel and the staffers he'd sent to the safe house. He was more a part of the team than he thought, she realized, feeling a faint beat of sadness that she wasn't part of anyone's team.

"There's more," he said. "And you're not going to like it."

She stared into the gathering darkness for a long moment before saying quietly, "They're out there waiting for us, aren't they?"

He nodded. "Yeah, I think so. Call it a gut instinct. Problem is, with all the rocky hills and caves just north of here, it'd be impossible for the cops to flush them out, even if they had the manpower. Robert and the other field agents might've been able to manage it, but they're not here." He paused. "The Vault is compromised, so we can't go back in. I think our best bet is to make a run for it."

She took a deep breath to settle the sudden queasiness in her stomach, and nodded. "I trust you."

He stared at her for a long moment, expression bleak. Finally, he said, "We'll move out once it's dark. I asked Blake to stash a vehicle for us. We'll need to make sure they keep us in sight long enough to know we're not headed to the safe house." He paused, not bothering to voice the obvious corollary, that if they were close enough to see, they'd be close enough to shoot. "I'm sorry. If there were any other way…" He trailed off, frustration evident in the long lines of his body, in the tension across his face and shoulders.

She shook her head. "They're not after you, or Evangeline's office staff. They're after me. They want me dead before I start remembering what I saw that day."

"Is any of it coming back?"

"Maybe." She blew out a breath, suddenly angry that there was a blank spot where the memory should have been. "At this point I don't know what's an actual memory and what's just wishful thinking. I can picture the helicopter and the guy with the rocket launcher, who I'm pretty sure is the same guy from the hospital. The build and clothes are right…at least I think they are. Maybe I'm projecting that, too." She closed her eyes and concentrated, which only made the hazy images seem less distinct. "There was a pilot wearing a headset, and someone sitting next to him, but I don't have any details on either of them."

"They were probably too far away for you to get a good look," Ethan said. He gave her hand a quick squeeze, and she was surprised to realize they were close together in the lee of the concealed doorway, nearly embracing as she gripped his forearm with one hand, while his opposite hand held hers. Their faces were very near, their bodies sharing warmth as the quick dusk fell around them. Heat shifted inside her. Need.

Overhead, the first star came to life, a poignant reminder that they weren't underground anymore.

"Thank you," she said softly. She closed the distance between them, until their breaths mingled on a warm puff of air as she said, "If

it hadn't been for you, I don't think we
would've made it out."

The darkness bound them together in that
moment, with the light of a single star twin-
kling down on them. She hesitated a moment,
giving him the chance to move away. Instead
he eased down to her as she eased up to him,
and their lips met in a moment of silent accord.

The kiss began as a soft touch of sensitized skin, a brush of warmth and moist air.
Then, as though he'd been waiting for the
moment, for the invitation, Ethan gave in to
her, leaned into her on a groan. And took.

His tongue swept into her mouth,
claiming, possessing, stamping his flavor on
each of her neurons as heat flared to life,
centered in her core and then spearing
outward to her fingertips, which held on to
him like a lifeline. She gasped at the sensa-
tions and he crowded closer, spinning them
until she had her back pressed against the
smooth metal of the concealed doorway.

Her full breasts melded to the hard wall of
his chest, chafing the aching want to a spiral
of pleasure. Lower down, she felt the hard
evidence of his desire and gloried in the sensation, in the promise. They strained

together, their kiss expanding from gratitude to something far bigger, far more important.

Excitement sizzled through Nic. She leaned into the kiss, sliding her hands up his chest to the sides of his face, where the skin of his cheeks and jaw was warm and stubble rasped beneath her palms.

"Wait. Nic, stop." He reached up and gripped her wrists as though he meant to push her away. Instead, he held her in place. Their faces were so close she could see the regret in his eyes when he said, "This doesn't mean what you think it means. It can't."

This time, instead of feeling hurt or disappointed, she felt a bite of anger. She pulled her hands away from his so she could shove at his chest. "You mean it could, but you won't let it."

"I'm not the man you think I am," he said, frustration evident in his tone, though both of them were speaking quietly, aware of the danger surrounding them. "I'm not a leader, and I'm sure as hell not somebody you want to depend on in a crisis."

"No," she countered, "you're afraid of letting anybody get too close to you." But as her hiss hung in the air, she had to wonder whether she was talking about him, or about herself. She was the one who'd closed herself off after Jonah left, focusing on a school project that nobody cared about except her and a handful of kids. She shook her head. "I'm sorry. You didn't deserve that. You're doing your best to—"

"Sh. Hear that?"

Nic froze, aware that he was shifting against her, easing her behind him as he drew his weapon, body tense. She pressed close to his back, trusting him with her safety, if not her heart. Straining to hear, she detected nothing at first. Then, the rattle of pebbles against stone.

Someone was sneaking down on them from above.

Spain

DAYLIGHT began to seep around the corners of the box truck's accordion door as a new day dawned. Evangeline sat with her back against the metal wall and her husband's head in her lap. Robert's eyes were closed and his breathing was even, but she knew he was only pretending to sleep. His body was too tense for repose, too ready to spring to action even though his muscles were weak after three days with no food or water.

That wariness was an invisible barrier between them, proof that he didn't trust her to keep watch, that he didn't trust her to do anything more than run the damn office. He was pretending to sleep because he was angry with her, furious that she'd allowed herself to walk into a trap. It didn't seem to matter to him that Cam and John had approved the plan—albeit reluctantly and with a great deal of heated argument on both sides—and the PPS team had agreed it was the only way to pinpoint Robert's location.

"And it worked, too," she whispered, figuring he wouldn't answer.

He surprised her by saying, "There was no guarantee, Evie. They could've taken you somewhere else. Hell, they could've killed you on the spot. Your name's on the damn list. Mine isn't."

She glanced down at him and saw that his eyes were still closed, but the lines beside his mouth cut deeper. She held in a sigh, and a beat of desperate sadness. Going into their marriage, she'd known that she and Robert had different concepts of equality, but it hadn't seemed important. She'd convinced herself the nearly twenty-year age gap was equally unimportant. Now she wondered if she'd let dreams get the better of logic. She and Robert had never disagreed so thoroughly before. Or maybe they had, and she'd been too ready to give in, thinking that peace equaled love.

Not anymore, she thought vehemently. She'd grown strong in the two years he'd been gone, and he would either have to learn to love her as the woman she'd grown into, or he'd have to—

She broke off there, unable to even think the alternative.

"I love you," Robert said suddenly, his voice tinted with sadness as though his thoughts had paralleled hers.

"I love you, too," she said, but let her head fall back against the wall of the box truck as she wondered whether love might not be enough for them.

Soon, she joined Robert in closing her eyes and pretending to sleep as the sun climbed in the sky. The box truck began to heat, and the hours ticked past. By noontime, Cam and John would have the others in place for the rescue, giving them a three-hour window before Clive's twenty-four-hour countdown expired.

Evangeline was nearly dozing when she heard the sound of footsteps crunching on gravel. Before she could react, Robert rolled and sprang to his feet, then pulled her up to stand behind him.

Her heart pounded into her throat as the lock rattled and the accordion door rolled up to reveal Clive and two of his thugs, all three armed and looking mean.

When Clive saw them both standing, poised to attack, he said, "Give me a good excuse. I dare you." Robert stayed where he was, and the bastard smirked. "Coward." He gestured with his weapon. "Come on, and no tricks. I'd love an excuse to waste both of you and get on with more important things."

Robert jumped down first, then turned back to help Evangeline out of the truck. When their eyes met, he mouthed, *Stay close and follow my lead.*

She didn't dare nod at him, but she did feel a little lift beneath her heart, a faint tendril of hope that he could keep them alive long enough for Cam and the others to catch up. Then she remembered something that had her knees buckling and a moan escaping from between her lips.

The GPS transmitter was still in the box truck. Cam wouldn't know where they'd been taken.

Colorado, USA

ETHAN'S HEART drummed against his ribs and adrenaline zinged through his bloodstream. Part of him itched for a chance to grab one of the bastards who'd been tracking Nic, but he couldn't. He was responsible for her safety, and that of their child.

For the first time, the thought brought a sense of bloody-minded determination rather than blind panic, but he couldn't think about that just then, because a shower of sand and small rocks cascaded down from above their hiding spot, and a muffled grunt warned that whoever was out there was only a few feet away.

Then a dusty, booted foot appeared from the right side of the earthen archway, followed by an equally dusty jeans-clad leg. Before the rest of the guy could appear, Ethan hissed, "Go!" and lunged.

He grabbed the man's legs in a flying tackle that sent them both sprawling onto the rocky ground.

Ethan recovered first, twisting and driving an elbow into the guy's gut. He got a quick impression of his opponent's face, and the heavy brows, wide cheekbones and thick lips jibed close enough with Nicole's description of her attacker at the hospital that a new burst of adrenaline, one that bordered on hatred, had him plowing his fist into the bastard's face.

"Ethan!" Nicole shouted. "Behind you!"

He spun and yanked up his gun, but was too late to deflect the second man, who caught him in the chest with a flying tackle that sent them both back to the ground. When they hit, Ethan's gun skidded across the packed dirt, out of reach.

What had been a pretty evenly matched fight moments before now became two-on-one, and threatened to turn real ugly, real quick. Ethan scrambled to his feet and backed toward the small opening that hid Nicole, trying to divide his attention between the two thugs, who advanced with fists raised and blood in their eyes.

"We've got to get out of here," Ethan said

quietly to Nic. "We're going to need a distract—"

A gunshot cracked from right behind him and the goon on the left went down hard, screaming and clutching his thigh. Shock froze the second guy for a second, and then he broke, grabbing his companion and dragging him off to the side of the archway.

Ethan spun, plucked his gun from Nic's limp fingers, took her hand and started running for the road. "Come on!"

Moments later, he saw that Blake had come through as promised. At the side of the paved strip, a dusty motorcycle leaned on its kickstand, neatly camouflaged beneath a sand-colored net.

"Take this." He tossed her one of the two helmets Blake had left, and yanked off the net. "Hope you're not afraid of bikes."

"I—I just shot a man." Eyes wild, she looked around, holding the helmet loosely in one hand.

"Here." Ethan snagged the helmet and stuck it on her head. A quick glance at the horizon showed no evidence of the two men, but the conspirators had already proven themselves smarter than average. They could easily be monitoring from afar. "Got your helmet? Climb on."

He waited until she was settled, then kicked the bike into action and peeled out onto the open road, leaving the camouflage net behind. For a brief moment, he thought they'd gotten away clean.

Then he heard a terrible noise, growing louder over the roar of the motorcycle's engine.

It was the sound of a helicopter, approaching fast.

Chapter Ten

As Ethan sent the motorcycle flying down the road, Nic wrapped her arms around his waist and locked her hands together so hard her fingers ached. Worse than the pain, though, was the feeling of exposure when she looked back in the fading light and saw a helicopter's silhouette and running lights appear over the ridge behind them and drop down, speeding along the winding tarmac, quickly closing the distance.

"Ethan!" she screamed, feeling as though the wind tore the words from her mouth.

"I know," he shouted. "Hang on!"

I am hanging on! she wanted to scream, but didn't have a chance, because moments later, he cut the bike hard and turned up a trail beside the road.

The single headlight beam showed that

they were in a narrow, rocky gulley. Nic hung on tight, but the jarring ride jolted her body against his and made her teeth rattle. Rocks spun out from beneath the tires and the engine note dropped to a growl, but they flew up the trail, accelerating away.

The black helicopter overshot and had to correct in a wide, sweeping turn that brought the chopper parallel to the bike. As Nic watched, a door rolled open in the side of the machine. The helicopter's dim interior lights silhouetted a man stepping out onto the runners and lifting a long, deadly-looking object onto his shoulder.

In a flash, the image was overlain with another memory, that of the same helicopter during daylight, hovering over the heart of Denver. A humming, rushing noise filled Nic's head and her vision telescoped to the face of the passenger sitting beside the pilot.

Then the memory was gone as though it had never been, and the wind noise and the engine's scream returned full force. Ethan yelled something, and she turned just in time to see that they were speeding toward a sheer rock face, only seconds away from impact.

She couldn't help it. She screamed, then

screamed again when she looked back at the chopper and saw a puff of smoke as the rocket launcher fired.

Dead. They were dead, and—

Ethan yelled and swerved the bike a half-second before they hit the sheer wall, sending them into a narrow crevice where two giant slabs of hill had separated to create a hidden tunnel. The faint light of dusk went out, plunging them into blackness lit only by the bike's headlight.

Then the rocket impacted behind them, and everything went red.

Terrified beyond screams, Nic vised her arms around Ethan's midsection. The shock wave hit, sending them hurtling forward, nearly out of control. Ethan cursed as he fought to keep the bike upright, wrestling to keep them on the narrow track that was bordered by jagged rock on either side.

Nic closed her eyes and pressed her helmeted face into his strong back, but she didn't pray. She trusted.

As if in answer, they shot back out into the open moments later, onto a wide swath of hardpan. There was a road leading away, but instead of accelerating, Ethan allowed the bike to slow, then brought it to a skidding halt and dropped his feet down to support them.

Not sure she believed what had just happened, Nic exhaled a shaky breath and straightened away from him, forcing her cramped fingers to unknot. He killed the engine, leaving them in a silence that seemed thunderously loud. Nic became aware of the quick thrum of blood in her ears, and the flush of exhaustion that followed an adrenaline rush.

They both pulled off their helmets and sat for a second, listening, but the only sounds not of nature were the tick of hot metal as the motorcycle cooled in the air of the gathering dusk, and the faint sound of rotor thumps fading in the distance.

"They're leaving," she breathed, unable to believe they'd made it.

"Probably figured they couldn't risk someone noticing that explosion." Ethan shifted so he was turned sideways on the bike, partway facing her. In the growing moonlight, she could see the lines of stress pulling at the corners of his eyes and mouth.

Neither of them said it aloud, but they both

knew the chopper had also gone because their pursuers thought they were dead. The concept was both terrifying and liberating— terrifying because they almost *had* died, liberating because it meant they were safe for the moment.

"Time to find ourselves a place to catch our breath and make a plan." Ethan faced forward on the motorcycle and brought the engine to life, his actions making her viscerally aware of the press of his muscular form against her body as she cuddled up behind him and gripped with her knees, freeing her hands to pull the helmet into place.

This time, when she slid her hands beneath his jacket to link across his midsection, and snuggled up behind him with her breasts pressed into the hard planes of his back, there was no panic in the movements. Instead, there was a gathering heat and a sizzle of chemical awareness that made her wonder if the draining adrenaline rush had redirected itself somewhere else entirely.

Then again, she thought as he sent them up the dirt track, headed to some unknown destination, who was she kidding? She didn't need adrenaline to want him, didn't need to be drunk or depressed, didn't need to be anything other than a healthy red-blooded woman in the presence of a man like *Ethan*. Or rather, in the presence of Ethan. Somewhere along the line, he'd become it for her.

And what the hell was she going to do about that?

BY THE TIME he'd turned the bike up the dirt track leading to Blake's mountain cabin, Ethan had stopped kidding himself about the logic of his choice. Yes, night was falling and the air was growing chillier by the minute, and it was true that even if the occupants of the helicopter thought to keep looking, they'd never think to look here. Thing was, he knew damn well there was a decent motel maybe fifteen miles down the mountain. He had enough emergency cash to rent a couple of rooms without using his credit card, and it might even have been a degree or two warmer on the ride down to the flatlands, but instead of turning toward the motel, he'd headed up, higher into the hills.

It wasn't logical, but it wasn't purely emotional either, he assured himself. It was, quite simply, what he'd wanted to do.

By the time they reached the cabin, clouds had gathered to obscure the moonlight, leaving the forest dark around them. When he turned the bike up the final stretch to the house, though, a bright motion-sensitive floodlight snapped on, illuminating the entire area with glaring white brilliance.

The cabin was a neat two-level structure, a mixture of stone and rough-hewn logs, with enough steel and glass to make it obvious that this was no rustic fishing cabin, despite the lake beyond. Knowing he was probably making a very big mistake and not sure he cared, Ethan rolled them around the side of the building, where a short breezeway led to an attached garage. He killed the engine, figuring he could put the bike away later.

Without the motor noise, the silence echoed in his eardrums, not unlike the way it had done just after the explosion that would've killed them if their luck had gone the other way.

At the thought, he kicked the bike up onto its stand and swung down, pulling his helmet off as he did so. "Come on. We'll get you warm inside."

He held a hand out to her, and when she took it, fine currents of electricity worked their way up his arm. Her fingers closed on his and she leaned into him as she climbed down off the bike, her movements more elegant than they should have been. With the temperature dip, she must've been cold, but instead of pale skin and chattering teeth, he saw a faint flush on her cheeks and a strange light in her eyes when she glanced at him, then away.

That light kindled something inside him, something he'd been staying one step ahead of for the past week, something he'd sworn not to let catch him.

Who was he kidding? he thought on a sudden burst of stark reality. If he'd really been running, he would've headed straight for that no-tell motel and rented two rooms. Instead he'd brought her here.

"Is this your place?" she asked, a tiny frown line forming between her eyebrows.

Ethan smothered a snort. "Not likely. It's Blake's. I've got an open-door invite, though." And he had a pretty good idea Blake probably intended to bring her up here as soon as they'd been dating for a decent interval. He was that sort of guy: a cordial meeting first, followed by flowers and a nice note, then a series of undemanding dates, picnics in the park, subtitled movies, that sort of thing. Then, when the time was right, a weekend away at his private mountain retreat. Blake was classy like that.

Unlike Ethan, who'd picked her up in a bar, slept with her then told her point-blank that he wanted nothing to do with the baby they'd created together.

The comparison killed the warmth her touch had created in his gut, making him wonder if his subconscious hadn't had another reason for him to bring her up to the cabin: to remind himself she deserved better. She deserved everything a guy like Blake could give her, and more.

"Are we going in or not?" she asked, and now he detected a faint tremor in her hands as she reached up to tuck a few dark curls behind an ear.

"Come on." He led the way up a stone-edged path, and for the first time, felt a pang of envy. The landscaping was just right, and the masonry and architecture fit together perfectly. As he opened the door and tapped the first code into the keypad of a sophisticated three-layer security system, then pressed his thumb to a scan pad, he thought about his townhouse. It had served him just fine for the past few years, but now it seemed too small as he typed in a second code, the door swung inward, and he ushered Nic into Blake's "little place in the mountains."

The lights had come up when he'd passed the final layer of security. The soft glow highlighted how utterly, perfectly she fit into the wide space of the main room, which reeked of taste and class. The polished-wood furniture was piled deep with soft pillows and down comforters, though there was little need for the latter, as a gas fire flickered in the corner, providing both warmth and ambiance.

Nic turned a full circle, and he saw her eyes light on the modern kitchen and the curving staircase that led to the loft-style upper level, which held the master suite and two guest rooms. When she finished her circuit and her eyes landed on him once again, her lips curved, this time all the way, and the laugh caught in her eyes. "With friends like these, who needs motels?"

"Blake is a good guy," Ethan said, the words seeming stiff and unnatural. "The shower upstairs is amazing, and he keeps a pretty decent collection of spare clothes on hand. Check the closet in the first guest room." He waved to the left side of the loft. "Something should fit. You go get warm. I'll make a few calls and pull some food together."

Her smile softened. "That sounds perfect. Thanks."

She turned and headed up the stairs, and the situation seemed so normal, so domestic, that for a moment he forgot who they were and what they were doing. He was halfway to the stairs before he realized that he'd moved. He forced himself to stop, to let her go up alone, but a part of him fought the hold, yearning to follow her and climb into the multi-jet shower, to continue what they'd begun ten weeks earlier.

"Phone call," he reminded himself. "Food."

Fifteen minutes later, he had a bare-bones meal thrown together from the staples in the cabinets and freezer, and he'd left Blake a heads-up that they were crashing in the cabin, but that was about all he'd managed. None of his calls had gone through to the PPS team in Spain, which worried the hell out of him. At the same time, he remained all too aware of what was going on overhead. It was too easy for him to picture Nicole naked in the shower, slick and wet and pink, soaping herself up, and—

"Get a grip and be a man." He punched the next string of numbers into his cell hard enough to make his index finger throb.

After three rings, Angel answered. "Hey, boss. We're here and all's quiet, except for Jerry snoring." She paused. "Oh, and the small detail that there's twenty of us and only one bathroom? We're either going to be very good friends or we're going to hate each other when this is over."

Ethan actually managed to crack a smile at that, but the expression faded quickly as he said, "Have you heard from Madrid?"

"Nothing. Damn. I was hoping Evangeline would've called you."

"They're probably busy," Ethan said, but he knew the excuse didn't play for either of them. "You guys manage to get any sort of information feed going yet?"

"The techs are working on it. We should have a secure Internet connection by morning."

"Good." Ethan thought for a moment, considering and rejecting investigative options. Problem was, there were too many possibilities and not enough good ones, now that the helicopter lead had played out. Or had it? There was one last thread to pull, he realized. "Once you're up and running, have the team concentrate on Rocky Mountain Sky helicopter tours. I want to know who's running the operation, who's funding it, who their five biggest clients are… Anything you think will help."

Even with the breach of the Vault and the subsequent chase, all they knew was that someone wanted Nic dead. They still didn't know who, damn it.

"I'm on it," Angel said, and for the first time since he'd met her, Ethan actually believed that she *was* on it.

"Call me if you hear from Madrid," he said. "Or if you need anything."

"We're fine," Angel replied. "Take care of yourself." She rang off, leaving Ethan standing in Blake's kitchen, awash in a strange, baffled sort of pride at how PPS's receptionist had stepped up, despite—or perhaps because of—the situation.

Evangeline had always said Angel was just waiting for an excuse to grow up. Apparently, she'd found it.

Upstairs in the loft, he heard the sound of movement, of doors opening and closing, and he forced himself not to imagine Nicole toweling herself off and getting dressed, forced himself not to picture helping her undress once again. It wasn't right and it wasn't fair. He owed it to Nic—and to the child she carried—to step back, step away and let her find the right man, one who'd be kind and treat her right. One she could depend on.

If he didn't, if he acted on his impulses now, that'd make him no better than his father, who'd done the family a favor by leaving when Ethan was eight. Hell, the bastard had done the family a disservice by staying that long.

The memory of his old man had Ethan clenching his fist and looking at it, seeing the similarities he'd tried so hard to avoid, and failing that, to outrun. He'd never considered himself a noble man, but maybe Angel wasn't the only one of Evangeline's projects who'd been looking for an excuse to grow up. Maybe he had been, too.

So, when he heard Nicole's footsteps, he told himself to be a man. Then he looked up and found her standing a few steps up the spiral staircase, wearing a thick fleece robe along with a pair of men's wooly socks that bagged at her ankles. Her hair was a damp profusion of near-black curls, and the robe almost swallowed her up. She would've looked like a waif, like something small and fragile if it weren't for her eyes. They were violet pools, warm and liquid and every bit those of the woman he'd met that night at Hitchin's. The woman he'd had to have, and damn the consequences.

It hadn't been the loneliness that'd drawn him to her, Ethan finally acknowledged deep inside as he stood rooted to the kitchen floor. It hadn't been the drink or the memories brought to the fore by a friend's wedding, which he'd ducked out of just after the I do's. Maybe all those things had been part of it, weakening his defenses just enough. But the loneliness and sorrow hadn't been what attracted him.

No, that had been the woman herself. That had been Nicole. Strong, elegant, self-possessed Nicole, who didn't value herself nearly enough, who didn't see what he saw.

Or maybe she did, he realized as she took two more steps down, so their eyes were level across the space separating them. The gleam of utter conviction in her expression said she knew exactly what she was worth, and exactly what she wanted. But didn't she realize that if she wanted him, the two were a contradiction?

"This is a bad idea," Ethan said finally, not bothering to pretend she'd come down for dinner. His words came out thick, forced through a throat that was suddenly clogged with emotion, with need and want crashing up against logic.

"Probably," she said with a fleeting smile that did strange things to his insides. "But at the moment I can't say I care." She paused. "You've made your position clear, as have I. But we're adults, too, and given the situation, I think it's only natural that we've gotten… close to each other, right?" She took a deep breath, and for the first time, he saw a hint of nerves in her eyes when she said, "So, what do you say? It's not like I can get pregnant all over again, and I…" She exhaled and twined her fingers together beneath the voluminous sleeves of Blake's robe. "I want this. I really do." She squared her shoulders and looked him straight in the eyes. "Don't you?"

Chapter Eleven

Ethan was still for so long, Nic thought he'd turned to stone, or worse, that she'd misread the signals. The heat of a blush climbed her cheeks, and she was just about to back down and stammer an excuse when he moved.

He crossed the distance between them, stopping at the base of the stairs. With her on the first step, they were eye level when he lifted his hands to frame her face and, without another word of protest, touched his lips to hers.

Where their first time had been tinged with alcohol, desperation and a faint sting of shame even as the heat had flared between them, now there was only the sizzling flame and the knowledge that they might not have a future, but they had one more night.

She eased up a step, wordlessly urging

him to follow her upstairs, where the master bedroom held a wide king-sized bed that was adrift in a forest-green comforter and scattered earth-toned pillows that had to have been a decorator's doing.

But instead of following her, Ethan eased away, caught the sash of her robe in one hand, and tugged her back down a step. Then another. Finally, he broke the kiss and, still without speaking, took her hand and led her to the main room, where the couches, thick-piled rugs and crackling fireplace offered another option for romance. He touched a wall unit in passing and brought the lights down, until the only illumination came from the firelight.

The yellow luminance gleamed off the side of his face and throat as he turned to face her. Before, she'd thought him solitary. Lonely. Now, she knew that he was a man who claimed solitude, yet looked after the people he considered his own. He led but didn't consider himself a leader, and he worked as a bodyguard, yet thought himself a failure as a protector.

He cocked his head, eyes pensive. "You're sure you want to do this?"

"Yes," she said without hesitation. "You?"

Jonah-the-jerk would've answered the question with something glib and poetic and meaningless. She expected that Ethan would simply kiss her rather than risk the words. Instead, he brought her hand to his lips. "It's been years since I've wanted anything as much as I want you right now."

Feeling the prick of tears at the sentiment, she let him draw her close, until they were standing face-to-face and the fire warmed one side of her. "I'm not half-drunk this time."

"Me neither." His brows quirked slightly. "Do you think it'll be as good as I remember?"

"Let's find out," she whispered, and they moved as if with one mind, meeting halfway in a kiss that started out a chaste promise, but quickly blossomed into an openmouthed exploration of lips and tongue and teeth, of playful nips and long, soul-searching kisses.

Nic moaned. Her head spun and her insides shimmered with hot, molten energy, a pulsing demand that had her crowding closer and lifting her hands to his clothing. The faintest hint of gasoline odor clung to him, a reminder of their harrowing motorcycle ride, and the heat that had ridden her since, the gut-wrenching physical awareness she could no longer deny. Working almost feverishly, she tugged at his shirt, laughing as he struggled to pull it off without breaking their kiss.

She would have liked to step back and look, to see the hard, heavy muscles she could feel beneath her fingertips, and the fine furring of hair across his upper chest, narrowing to a point that disappeared into the waistband of his jeans. But the urgency building between them—in their kisses and caresses, in the moans and whispered words of praise—in that heat, there was no time to step back and look.

Their kisses turned hot and wet and full of intent. Ethan murmured something that sounded like her name, or maybe an endearment, and loosened the knot of her sash. She shivered as he ran his hands over her hips and up her lower back, and a shimmer of want followed his caress. The skin of her breasts tightened, crinkling her nipples into hard buds that ached with desire. She pressed closer to ease the ache, humming with pleasure at the feel of skin on skin.

Ethan drew out his kisses until she felt as though she was floating a few inches off the floor, wrapped in a soft, sensual mist that concentrated every touch, every whisper, every slide of tongue or scrape of tooth in her center, where the heat coiled tight and greedy.

There was no hesitation in him now, no questioning or reserve. There was only his potent male flavor and the sure stroke of his hand and the sound of his voice when he broke off the kiss, leaned his forehead against hers and said, "I looked for you."

She blinked up at him. "When?"

"After that night. I went back to Hitchin's, hoping someone knew you."

Foolish warmth curled through her. "That was a one-time thing. I'd never been there before, never since." But it mattered that he'd tried.

"Your number's not listed." He shrugged. "Didn't seem like you wanted to be found."

She blinked against a suspicious hint of moisture, unwilling to admit how much his efforts, however small, had touched her. "Consider me found."

This time, she initiated the kiss, sinking

into him and tugging him down. He pulled a comforter from one of the couches and followed her until they lay together on the blanket-covered rug. His hands found their way beneath her robe, then cupped her hip and urged her closer, and closer still, until he trailed his fingers up her torso, dancing across her ribs. She arched against him, offering more, demanding more.

When he only stroked a long, lazy line between her breasts and across her belly, she growled in mock frustration and broke the kiss long enough to say, "Tease me, will you? We'll see about that."

Her words surprised a chuckle out of him, but the laugh ended on a groan when she worked her own fingers down the taut muscles of his abdomen to his waistband, where she dipped her fingers just barely into the warmth beyond.

There, she paused, tracing small circles in a tease of her own, one that had him pressing against her hand in silent entreaty. That gesture and the taste of him, along with the look of exquisite torture on his rough-hewn face, brought power welling up in her alongside heat.

With Ethan, she felt sexy and adventurous in a way she never had with Jonah. With Ethan, she felt safe and protected in a way she never did alone.

With Ethan, she didn't feel alone at all, and therein lay danger.

Not now, she told herself, shoving aside the faint threat of wistfulness and flinging herself into the moment, into the heat they made together.

Where before there had been a hasty, alcohol-blurred race to strip and grapple together, now there was time for touching and tasting. More importantly, where before it had been all flash and flame laced with an edge of the forbidden, two strangers brought together by quick attraction and nothing else, now they knew each other. They were friends in a way, bound by shared experiences, by danger, and yes, by the child she carried.

There was another level now, Nic realized as she undid the button of his jeans and slid the zipper down, baring him to her touch. They might not be making love or making a future, but this was way more than sex.

It had to be, she thought, arching into his touch as his teasing fingers stroked up to cup her breast, his touch gentle yet sure. It had to be more, because that was the only way to explain the heavy pressure in her chest and her core, where heat met emotion and the two together formed a molten ball that was something more than need, something less than love.

At least she hoped it wasn't love. She'd been down that path before, and knew that wasn't where she and Ethan were headed. They were headed only to where they were that moment.

It would have to be enough.

Humming with the feel of his clever fingers bringing her nipple to a peak, she reached inside his open jeans to touch the length of him, where iron hardness cloaked in warm, achingly soft skin jerked lightly be-neath her fingers, with the beat of his heart.

At that, he tore his mouth from hers and pressed his cheek against her temple, his breath quick and hot against her skin. "Nicole," he said, with a faint hitch in his voice that made her heart take a long, lazy roll in her chest.

"Ethan?" she said in return, and reached

up to cup his jaw and press his face against hers.

"I wish…" He trailed off, then said, "I want…" He inhaled a long breath, one that expanded his chest and pressed them closer together. "Aw, hell, sweetheart." His voice was low and throbbed with emotion, and when she leaned back away from him so she could see into his eyes, she found that same emotion looking back at her. Desire mixed with something else, something warmer and far less sure.

Its twin shimmered to life within her, love laced with a fear that had her shifting to touch a finger to his lips. "Hush. We'll figure it out later."

When he closed his eyes and pressed a kiss to her fingertips, she took it as agreement. Acceptance. There would be a later for them. There had to be. It was too good between them to walk away, whatever the difficulties.

"There's only one problem," she said.

"What?"

"You're wearing too many clothes." She grinned and tugged at his jeans, and he rolled onto his back to fish out his wallet for a condom before he stripped off his pants. She lay still and watched him, loving how the firelight played across the taut muscles of his chest and arms, and how it warmed her face and the skin of her breasts and belly, which were bare where he'd parted the robe and pushed it aside.

When he rolled back to her, gloriously naked, he paused lying on his side, facing her. Looking at her as she had looked at him.

At any other point in her life, with any other man, Nic would have flushed and covered herself. But now, with him, she only smiled. "Like what you see?"

He started to speak and broke off, shaking his head. When he spoke again, it was simply to say, "Yes."

Then he leaned down to her, angling himself atop her, and touched his lips to hers, nearly breaking her heart with the gentleness, with the sentiment he couldn't express but they both felt. They came together on a shared sigh, a mingling of breath that became a kiss, a kiss that became an embrace, and an embrace that became even more as he finally slipped the robe from her shoulders, leaving it to pool beneath them, cushioning her hips as he came down atop her, aligning them heat to heat, center to center.

She parted her legs to accept him, baring her most sensitive folds to the fire-warmed air and the good solid press of his hard flesh.

Twined together, not sure where one left off and the other began, they kissed endlessly, tasting each other, learning each other until Nic could've sworn their hearts beat in time. Then he shifted and slid a hand between them, touching her intimately, rubbing the nub of her pleasure until everything tightened inside her, coalescing to a single knot of sensation. She cried out against his mouth as he kissed her in unison with his touch, his tongue mimicking the action of his clever fingers.

Always before she'd struggled to reach the peak, laboring toward it like a destination rather than a bonus. So when she came in a rush, she nearly yelled with the pleasure of it, the effortless surprise of it. The waves of sensation washed over her without warning, tugging her under with them and then pushing her out the other side, where every cell of her body throbbed on a wholly new level of sensitivity, a higher plateau of pleasure than she'd ever known before.

When she could breathe again, when she could see again, she realized she had her eyes open, and that she and Ethan were looking at each other. Into each other.

"Wow," she said, not even making an attempt at glibness. "Can I have another one of those?" When he cracked a smile and the shadows fled from his eyes, she said, "Better yet, do you want one, too?"

"I wouldn't say no," he retorted, and rolled onto his back, so that his proud, jutting flesh was silhouetted against the firelight. But when he tore open the foil packet, she took the condom from him.

"Allow me."

She heard his hiss of indrawn breath as she leaned over him, the firelight warm against her naked skin, her hair falling forward to brush against his taut stomach as she took him into her mouth, laving him, loving him. He muttered something low and guttural at the back of his throat and his hand slid from her hip to the thick rug, where his fingers dug in as he hung on for the ride.

She worked him, sliding her lips and tongue along the wide, pulsing vein on the underside of his hard length, then across the soft, bulbous tip until she sensed his control was near breaking. Then, only then, she covered him with the protective sheath and moved to straddle him, rising up above him while firelight crackled across her bare skin.

That impulse, too, was a surprise. Where before she'd been, if not passive, then not aggressive, now she took control, took him into her body and gloried in the sharp pressure within, the sensation of being filled, of being joined.

Seeming to know what she needed, perhaps even before she did, Ethan dug his fingers into the soft nap of the rug, holding himself still, letting her take command, at least for the moment. His eyes were heavy-lidded, his face taut with an expression that hovered between pleasure and exquisite torture, but he watched her rise above him, watched her make love to him.

Heat, along with a warm, spiraling hope, swirled inside her, tightening as she rode him higher and higher. Then, in a flash, he broke from compliance, yanking his hands from the rug onto her hips and rearing up so they were face-to-face, chest-to-chest. He kissed her, not roughly as the fire in his eyes would have suggested, but so thoroughly it blocked out everything else, until he was the only thing in her world—the feel of him, the taste of him.

She was only peripherally aware that he'd spun them, neatly reversing their positions so she had her back pressed against the rug as he pressed himself onto her, into her. The needs coiled hard and hot, rushing her to a second peak as he pressed his hot cheek against hers and thrust into her. She met him stroke for stroke, giving as much as she took. A groan reverberated in his chest, or maybe a growl. The low, feral sound echoed inside her, calling to something more powerful than she'd ever known before. She felt like a temptress, a goddess. Powerful.

Riding that wave, she arched against him and raked her fingers across his back and ribs on either side, with just enough fingernail to have him shuddering against her and driving home hard to touch her core.

She gasped and grabbed on to him, and then it was a race to the peak, with each of them goading the other on, chasing each other, pushing each other until Nic's breath rattled in her lungs and then left her in a rush. Pleasure gripped her, locking her muscles and concentrating her entire being on the place where they were joined, where the hot, hard friction suddenly contracted and then flung outward, blasting through her in a shock wave of delight that had her keening his name, gripping his shoulders and hanging on for the ride.

He thrust into her again and again, prolonging the pleasure, driving it higher until her vision grayed and she came again. He followed her over with a harsh groan that rattled deep in his chest and ended on the whisper of her name.

They stayed locked together for a long moment, tangled in each other, as their heartbeats leveled off. Then Ethan rolled, carrying her with him to nestle in the crook of his arm as they both concentrated on breathing.

We should talk, Nic thought, knowing that too much was still unsaid. But she was warm and replete, and the crisp crackle of the fire counterpointed the steady thud of his heartbeat. Those sounds, along with an overwhelming sense of rightness, of being exactly where she was meant to be, combined to send her under.

Instead of talking, they slept.

Spain

ROBERT KNEW he should've died two years earlier, in a Pyrenees plane crash. Now, as Clive led him and Evangeline across a deserted road and up to a run-down cottage, he realized it was good that he was both alive and already dead. It meant he wouldn't hesitate when the time came.

If one of them was making it out of Spain, it was damn well going to be her.

As if she heard his thoughts, she glanced over at him and shook her head in warning. *We're in this together,* her expression said.

He snorted inwardly at the thought, then nearly missed a step. Oh, hell. That was what she'd been saying for the past month, wasn't it? She'd accused him of not seeing her as an equal, as part of his team.

She was right, he thought on a clutch of dismay.

"Keep it moving," the guy behind him growled, punctuating the order with a sharp pistol jab. "We haven't got all day."

Robert stumbled forward, his feet moving automatically while connections were made in his brain.

She'd waited for him, as he'd known she would, but she hadn't been sitting at home, pining for him. She'd been keeping the business going. Hell, she'd grown the damn company, hiring new operatives and expanding their client base. More than that, she'd set out to make a difference, taking on projects like Angel and Ethan. She'd built a life for herself without him in it.

And that had been one of his sticking points, he realized. Somewhere deep inside, he'd wondered whether part of her resentment had been because she'd gotten used to life without him, maybe even preferred it.

He'd been afraid, he realized as Clive and the thugs shoved them up the steps of the run-down cottage. Afraid that she'd been getting ready to move on when he'd returned, that she hadn't known how to tell him that their marriage was over.

He glanced at her now, and his heart constricted at the look she sent him, part entreaty, part resentment. Both emotions found twins inside him, making him face the fact that he'd been acting like an idiot. Heck, never mind acting, he'd *been* an idiot. He should've kept in closer contact with her, should have shared the burden of their separation.

In protecting her, he'd shut her out.

"I love you, Evie," he said aloud, not caring who heard. "I shouldn't have disappeared on you. I should've let you in."

That earned him a sharp jab from the guy behind him, who snapped, "Shut up and keep it moving."

More importantly, though, it earned him a quick look and a tentative smile from his wife. A swift touch of her hand against his when she faked a stumble and bumped into him.

"Knock it off," the guy behind Robert growled, shoving them into a small whitewashed room with a single narrow, barred window. The only furnishings were a small table that held a laptop computer, and a single rolling chair.

"Sit," Clive ordered Evangeline. "Read what's written on the screen."

Realizing that the other two had waited outside, Robert shifted position, waiting for his chance.

Evangeline sat and stared at the screen for a moment, her shoulders tightening. Clive snapped, "Read it aloud. The camera's on."

Which meant the laptop was recording the scene, but to what end? Was it so Clive could replay the scene as many times as he wanted, reliving the moment he finally defeated his former student? Or was there someone else involved, someone who even now was watching from a remote location?

"My name is Evangeline Prescott," she read, her voice inflectionless with anger, and perhaps fear. "I herewith confess to masterminding the murder of film star Nick Warner and conspiring with Peter Turner in a land-trust pyramid scheme designed to give us control of the oil rights in and around Hank Ward's ranch in Colorado. My beloved husband, Robert Prescott, was also involved in—" She broke off suddenly and turned to Clive. "Who wrote this crap? It doesn't sound anything like me. I don't use words like *herewith*, and right now I'd be just as likely to conk Robert on the head for being a stubborn mule than call him *my beloved*. Honestly!" She huffed out a breath and deliberately turned her back to her husband.

In the moment of silence following her snarl, Robert heard a quiet scraping sound coming from the other side of the wall, beneath the barred window.

"Damn it, woman," he shouted, cranking the volume to cover Cam and the others. "I stay hidden for two damn years to protect you, and when I finally manage to come back, all I get is a nasty attitude."

Clive gestured again with his weapon. "Just read it already." Now he pointed his gun directly at Robert. "Or would you rather I just shot your husband right here and now?"

The seconds ticked down in Robert's gut. Nine… eight…seven…

"Fine." Evangeline turned back to the screen with a grimace. "My name is Evangeline Prescott, and—"

A sharp whistle pierced the quiet outside. Clive jerked at the sound, and that break in his concentration was all Robert needed. He lunged toward Evangeline even as she overbalanced the chair and hit the floor with her hands over her ears. Robert landed atop her, shielding her with his body as everything exploded around them.

The whitewashed walls blew with a roar and Clive and his thugs went flying. The table overturned and the laptop crashed to the floor. Robert held on to Evangeline as debris peppered his back in stinging pellets and the roar faded to a growl, then to silence.

Clive recovered first, scrambled to his feet and headed for the hallway, where his thugs were struggling upright. "Kill them!" he shouted, and bolted through the door.

The thugs gained their feet and rushed Robert as he pulled Evangeline up. Sunlight streamed onto both of them through a gaping hole in the wall.

"You take Clive," Evangeline ordered. "I can handle these two."

Robert gave a sharp nod. "I know you can." He pressed a quick, hard kiss to his wife's mouth, and bolted after the man who'd once been his friend and mentor, and was now his sworn enemy.

Chapter Twelve

Evangeline stood for a moment, stunned by Robert's quick acquiescence. Then she grinned, joy blooming through her as Fuentes's thugs closed on her, their weapons lost in the blast, their eyes narrowed with bloodlust and a determination that barely flickered when Cam and John flanked her, weapons drawn.

"Keep them alive," she ordered. "We'll want some answers."

When the first man lunged, she stepped back and let her men have at it, knowing they were stronger and better trained than she. Despite what Robert thought, she knew when to back down in a dangerous situation.

Cam took the first punch on his cleft chin, and the blow had his head snapping back on his neck. He stood fast, shook his head, and waded in, fists flying. Half a second later, John engaged the second thug with a war whoop. Both of the PPS operatives had identical feral grins on their faces and bloodlust in their eyes.

They needed this, Evangeline knew, needed finally to have a flesh-and-blood opponent to fight rather than the string of shadow games they'd been forced to play over the past few months.

Leaving Cam and John to their fight, she slipped through the deserted cottage. Instinct led her out the front door and across the street and through a barren field to the vine-draped box truck where she and Robert had been held. There, Robert and Clive were facing off.

"I trusted you," Robert said between gritted teeth, burying his fist in Clive's gut. The blow slammed Fuentes into the side of the box truck. "You were one of the good guys, damn it!"

He plowed his fist into Clive's jaw, but the wily old man ducked the next punch, deflecting Robert's fist into the box truck's metal wall. Robert howled and reeled back.

Clive's lip was split and his face bore reddened patches that would soon go to bruises. He was no longer gloating as he'd been since grabbing Evangeline at the Madrid airport. Instead, when he pressed himself against the box truck and looked wildly from side to side, she saw panic and calculation, and beneath that, a dull resignation.

The victory should have filled her with vicious joy, but she felt hollow when Robert turned his back on her, and dealt the bastard another punishing blow, making the fight into man against man, rather than the team against their enemy.

Despair welled up out of nowhere, or perhaps out of the place she'd been pretending didn't exist, the place that said their marriage had died two years earlier.

Back then, she'd had hope. She'd held on to it for longer than her friends thought wise, longer than maybe she should have. She'd told Ethan to move on, but now she was beginning to think she was the one who'd needed that advice.

Finally beginning to believe she'd lost Robert, that there was no hope for them, she turned away from the sight of her husband systematically pummeling the man who'd taught him to be a spy, the man who, in more ways than one, had taught him to depend on no one but himself.

Tears pressed as she walked away.

She'd barely reached the edge of the road when she heard footfalls chasing after her.

"Wait." Robert's voice was ragged with exertion, with emotion. "Evie, wait."

She stopped but didn't turn. "What is it?"

A large, foolish part of her hoped he'd say the right things, that he'd finally get it. But if he hadn't gotten it in the weeks he'd been back, why would he now? Men like him didn't change—it'd just taken her too long to see it.

"I'm sorry."

"For what?"

"For—" He broke off. "Look, can you at least turn around?"

She turned, and her heart clutched at the sight of him. Even wearing the ragged clothes of his captivity, he was gorgeous—all male, all arrogant and alpha. But there was something in his eyes, something she hadn't seen there before. Not uncertainty, precisely, but close. That flicker of vulnerability had a glow of hope lighting in her chest.

She took a step toward him. "Sorry for what?"

He inhaled, nostrils flaring, looking faintly trapped. He was quiet so long she thought he wasn't going to say anything, thought she'd lost him after all, but he finally exhaled and said, "I'm sorry I didn't trust you."

Ouch. Evangeline fought to hide the instinctive flinch. She'd known it, heck she'd thrown it at him once or twice, but hearing him come out and say it still hurt.

"I didn't trust you enough to let you in on what was happening," he continued, hands fisted at his sides. "I should've told you everything. I thought I was protecting you, but I was really protecting myself, and that wasn't fair."

"No," she said faintly. "It wasn't."

She was vaguely aware that John stood nearby, keeping watch on Clive's still form. He stayed close enough to help if Clive had reinforcements, far enough away to give the illusion of privacy as his bosses…what? What were they doing? Saving their marriage? Ending it?

No! a voice said deep inside Evangeline at the very thought, and for the first time in a long time, she knew what she *wasn't* doing.

She wasn't ending it, and she sure as hell wasn't going to let Robert end it.

She loved him.

"To hell with it," she said. "I'm not letting what happened—or what didn't happen— keep screwing up what we have together. I love you, damn it, and I know damn well that you love me, too."

A shudder ran through his long frame, and he said, "That was supposed to be my line. I was working up to it. I had the whole thing planned out."

Evangeline shrugged and laughter threatened to bubble up in her throat, where tears had been only moments earlier. "So I got there first. Deal with it."

"I will," he said. "I am." He exhaled a long sigh and opened his arms to her. "I'm sorry I shut you out sometimes. I promise to work on it."

Which, in her mind, was far better than him promising never again to turn away from her. That would've been an empty promise. But this…

This was a beginning. A fresh start.

A huge grin spread across her face as she stepped into her husband's arms. She pressed her face against his chest. She felt the sure, steady beat of his heart beneath his torn shirt, and felt the leashed power of his body. But for the first time since his return, she didn't feel as though his strength diminished hers.

For the first time, she felt stronger with him than without him.

She pulled back and looked up at him, then reached up and touched her lips to his. The kiss was no more than a brush of skin against skin, fleeting as a hummingbird's wings, but promising so much more to come.

When she pulled back, she hummed with pleasure and looked beyond him, to where John had bound and gagged Clive, no doubt leaving Cam to do the same to the other thugs. Then she glanced at her husband. "What now, boss?"

He tipped his head. "You tell me. They're your men."

And it was true, she realized. They *were* her men. Her responsibility. Her strength.

More than that, far more to the girl who'd grown up in and out of the foster system, they were her family.

She nodded, masking the leap of joy, and said, "Let's go home."

Colorado, USA

ETHAN AWOKE slowly, which was unusual for him. Even more unusual, he wasn't alone.

It took him a moment to process the warmth of the woman beside him, and the unfamiliar furnishings that came into focus as he blinked against the light of a new day.

Then things clicked into place with a one-two punch. One, he was in a guest room at Blake's mountain cabin. Two, he was sharing the bed with Nicole.

Despite all of his empty promises and vows, despite his best intentions, they'd come together twice in front of the fire, and once again after they dragged themselves, kissing and groping amidst half-hysterical laughter, up to the guest room.

The sex had been amazing, even better than before, now that they'd gotten to know each other and—

He broke off the train of thought. *Don't go there.* She was home and hearth, he was casual, fly-by-night. He wasn't good husband material, and he certainly wasn't a suitable father for a child who deserved nothing but the best.

Like the best that currently surrounded them, he thought with a wince, knowing he'd been on the right track with the idea of hooking her up with Blake. They'd be good together, he told himself firmly, being careful not to look at her, careful not to remember how her fingers had felt on him, how her lips—

He lunged from the bed, fists clenched at his sides. Standing naked in the middle of the room, he cursed himself for being stupid. Being weak. He should've stayed the hell away from her, should've done anything but what he'd done.

"Ethan?" Her voice was low and sweet, and furred with sleep. She rolled from her stomach onto her side and sat partway up, the sheet slipping off one shoulder and baring the upper slopes of her breasts.

When he realized he was staring, he snapped his eyes up to hers. "Sorry."

Her lips curved in a sensual, almost feline smile. "Don't be." But when he didn't respond, when he just stood there, her smile dimmed and a twist of pain entered her eyes. "Oh. Oh, boy." She sat up all the way and dragged a blanket over her shoulders until it cocooned her entire body, leaving only her face visible, and those dark, hurting eyes. "You're kidding me."

It seemed as though they'd had an entire conversation in that one look, but he couldn't argue with the conclusion she'd reached. He could only stand there, buck-naked and feeling like a complete jerk when he said, "I didn't mean for this to happen, Nicole."

He expected tears, dreaded them. Instead, her eyes blazed and she snapped, "Oh, please. Spare me the martyr routine." She wadded up one of the blankets and threw it at him. "Cover yourself. You've got to be freezing."

He caught the blanket on the fly and wrapped it around his waist even as he bristled. "It's not martyrdom to want the best for my child."

"Which I'm guessing, in your brain, is *not* you," she said with some asperity. "How about you trust me to have an opinion on that? The way I see it, this is *my* baby, *my* decision. Unless, of course, the whole I-wouldn't-make-a-good-father thing is just an easy excuse."

Anger kindled low in his gut, alongside something that felt surprisingly like fear. He rounded on her, close to snarling. "There's nothing easy about any of this, damn it! Don't you get that?"

"Frankly, no, I don't." She thrust her chin out, defiance warring with upset in her eyes. "Why don't you explain your reason to me?"

"Reasons," he corrected. "There are two reasons why I'd be no good for you or the baby. First, because I know what it's like to live with someone like me, and second because you can't depend on me."

She rose and crossed the room to stand in front of him. "What do you mean, 'someone like you'?" Her eyes glittered with anger, but her voice was almost soft when she said, "You say you're not a leader, but you got us all out of the Vault safely."

"A leader doesn't automatically make a good father," he said, hearing a faint thread of desperation in his voice.

"No, but a kind, brave and honorable man does." She lifted a hand to touch his cheek in the barest of caresses. "I believe in you, Ethan. When are you going to start believing in yourself?"

"You don't know me," he said sharply, the

words coming out far harsher than he'd intended. "Just because we've slept together a couple of times and we've spent some time together doesn't mean you know me, that you know what I'm capable of." He glanced down at his hands, which were fisted so tightly his knuckles ached. "My father—my biological father, that is—was a hard man, Nicole. He wasn't abusive, but we knew he didn't want to be there, didn't want to be a part of the family. I grew up tiptoeing around him, trying to make him want to be home, because I could see how much it meant to my mother."

Nicole let her hand drop away from his face, leaving a cool spot where his skin had been warm. Her voice was crisp when she said, "I'm not asking you for marriage, Ethan. I'm just asking you to give what's between us a chance."

"I can't," he said, desperation welling up and pressing on his lungs.

"You mean you won't."

Her eyes had gone cool and dismissive, and though that was what he'd wanted, some part of him couldn't let it end this way. He needed to make her understand.

He took a deep breath, then let it out again. "I was married before."

She nearly hid the wince, but her voice went cool. "What happened?"

"She died." The words didn't even begin to encompass what had happened, but he couldn't force the explanation past his gritted teeth, past the knot of guilty regret twisting in his gut.

"I'm sorry." But Nic shook her head. "I know this is going to sound callous, and I'm sorry about that, too, but I was engaged and the bastard cheated on me. I'm not saying that's better, but at least your wife didn't have a choice about leaving you. More importantly, I haven't let Jonah's behavior rule my life."

"Haven't you?" Ethan couldn't stop himself from saying. "It seems to me that you celebrated the one-year anniversary of your dead engagement by picking up a stranger in a bar."

"And I'm not letting how that turned out run my life either," she fired back, then paused before she said, "I'm trying to give us a chance, Ethan. I'm asking you to do the same."

Panic battered at the back of his throat.

Desperation. The feeling of sinking and not knowing when or where he was going to hit bottom. "Caro didn't just die," he said finally, the words leaving an old, bitter taste in his mouth. Like tears. Like blood. "I killed her."

Any other woman might have gasped in shock, or snapped an immediate denial, but not Nicole. She simply lifted her chin. "Tell me."

He couldn't *not* tell her, not with the memories crowding so thick around him he could barely see straight. "I'd just finished my tour of duty, had my discharge papers in hand. We were living in Vegas then, because that's where I'd been stationed, and we headed out to the strip to celebrate. You know, hit a casino, take in a show, all the silly things the locals hardly ever do." He blew out a breath, smelling the damp air, seeing the wet streets glittering beneath a thousand neon lights. "The other driver was drunk. He crossed the yellow line and cut all the way across my lane, doing sixty, maybe seventy. I swerved the wrong way." He closed his eyes against the remembered jolt, the crunch of impact and the powder blast of the air bags. "The guy hit the passenger side. If I'd just kept going straight…" He trailed off, having learned long ago that there was no such thing as "if only."

"And that's why you think it's your fault?" Nic said slowly. "Because you swerved the wrong way?"

"No. It's my fault because I moved her."

He'd been stunned for the first thirty seconds or so after the crash, maybe he'd even blacked out, he wasn't sure. The first thing he remembered was seeing Caro's face, her eyes open and scared. The first thing he remembered doing was reaching for her, trying to pull her toward him.

And the light in her eyes had gone out.

"I was a medic," he said, tipping his head back in an effort to force the grief back down where it belonged. "I damn well knew better, but I panicked. And because I panicked, she died right there, in my arms."

"I'm not going to bother telling you that it was a natural reaction, and that you shouldn't blame yourself for something you did while you were probably half-conscious," Nicole said softly, pain echoing in her words. "I'm sure you've heard all that before. So instead, let me ask you a question. Why does that make you a bad candidate for father-hood?"

Anger was a bitter taint at the back of his tongue as he snapped, "If you don't want to get it, I can't make you."

Matching rage flared in her eyes. "And if you want to use your wife's death as an excuse to keep coasting, I can't stop you."

He gritted his teeth and steeled himself against the glint of tears, telling himself it was better this way. There would be no more second chances for them after this. "Are we done here?"

She looked at him for so long, her eyes so sad, that he thought she'd try again.

Instead, she simply nodded. "Yeah, we're done."

SHE WATCHED him walk out of the room and knew in her heart that he was walking out of her life. And yes, that was probably overdra-matic, but she figured she was due for some drama after the week she'd had. Was still having.

"So deal with it," she said aloud, swiping her hands across her eyes and refusing to shed another tear. "He's just as big an idiot as Jonah was, only in a different way. I'm better off without him." She touched her stomach beneath the draped sheet. "*We're* better off without him."

Only she didn't feel better off as she showered in the guest bathroom, and when she opened the door and found her clothes in a neatly folded pile, she nearly crumbled.

Instead, she gritted her teeth, pulled on the clothes and strode downstairs with her chin up.

Ethan met her at the bottom of the stairs, fully dressed, with a cell phone pressed to his ear and a triumphant gleam in his eyes. He waved for her to wait as he ended the call with, "You bet. I'm going to swing back to the Vault to pick up my Jeep, and then I'll meet you at the safe house." Then he snapped the phone shut and said, "Robert and Evangeline are safe. Even better, they got Clive, and he's all but confessed to masterminding everything." He grinned at her, though shadows remained in his eyes. "It's all coming together. They flew through the night and landed a few minutes ago. With Clive's information, the cops should be able to round up the last of his secondaries by the end of the day."

"That's fantastic." Nic tried to inject enthusiasm into her voice, but all she felt was numb. It was over. In a few hours she and Ethan would say their goodbyes.

How had she miscalculated so badly? She'd been so sure the night before had been the start of something wonderful. Not a mistake. Not an ending.

But though Ethan might be a leader, he was also, deep down inside, an emotional coward. He thought it was better to rebuff connections than to take a risk, better to be alone than be vulnerable. He might tell himself he was making sacrifices to protect her from his bad decisions, to protect the baby from a bad childhood, but in the end he was simply protecting himself.

Well, he was right about one thing, Nic told herself firmly. She could do better than him. She didn't need a man who made her fight tooth and nail for every small emotion, and the baby could do better than a man who didn't want to be part of their family.

So she lifted her chin and said, "Good. Let's go. The sooner we get this over with, the sooner I can get back to my real life."

The words *without you* hung suspended in

the air between them until a soft chiming noise broke in, followed by the crunch of tires.

Someone had found them.

Chapter Thirteen

Ethan spun and reached for the 9 mm he'd tucked into his waistband, then relaxed when a quick glance at the video monitor beside the door showed Blake's silver BMW.

Ethan knew he should be relieved by his friend's arrival. The fact that a spurt of irritation tightened his chest with a possessive, jealous burn only served to remind him how badly he'd messed up. The more he'd tried to stay away from her, the more he'd wanted to be near her, until last night, when he'd made a huge mistake and wound up with her stuck inside his mind, inside his—

No, he thought quickly. Not his heart. Never in his heart, which is why he'd been right to end things between them.

"Stay here," he ordered, but was unsurprised when she followed him out the door.

Blake climbed out of his Beemer looking tall and handsome and rich as sin in creased jeans and cowboy boots, an open-necked shirt and a leather bomber that probably cost more than Ethan's mortgage.

Ethan stopped opposite the other man and forced himself to smother a spurt of resentment. "Hey. Hope you don't mind us crashing here last night."

"Of course not. *Mi casa* and all that." Blake's eyes went beyond Ethan. "Morning, Miss Benedict."

Ethan sensed her smile, and it put his back up, as did the lilt in her voice when she said, "It's Nic, remember?"

"Of course…Nic," Blake said, voice light, but when he turned back to Ethan, the teasing glint left his eyes. He nodded to the beat-up motorcycle, which still sat in the driveway. The formerly gleaming black-and-chrome bike was dust-covered and dented. "Looks like you had some trouble getting up here. What can I do to help?"

Ethan wanted to say he had it under control, but that would only prolong the inevitable, so he said, "I'd like you to hang with Nicole for the rest of the day."

"You want me to be a bodyguard?" Blake's grin was quick, but gave a glimpse of steel beneath, a hint of the warrior Ethan had come to know and respect the year before. "I thought that was your gig."

"Consider these special circumstances." In more ways than one, Ethan thought. He didn't dare turn and glance over at Nicole, didn't dare see what was in her eyes at the knowledge he was ditching her ahead of schedule. "Besides, the priority level is down—we've got the head scum and now we're just mopping up the grunts. It should take a day, maybe two. I want you to make sure nobody hassles her until you get the all clear from me."

Apparently catching some of the tension in the air, Blake glanced at Nicole. "That sound okay with you?"

Her shoulders stiffened beneath her bedraggled clothing, her chin lifted, and she didn't even look at Ethan before she said, "Sounds perfect. I'm looking forward to spending some more time with you."

The words were innocent enough, the edge beneath them anything but.

Blake tipped his head as though acknowledging both. "If you want to grab your stuff, we can head out now. We'll stay at my place—it's the safest option." He glanced at Ethan. "Is it cool for us to swing by her place so she can change?" He quirked an eyebrow in her direction. "No offense intended, of course."

"None taken. I'd love to go home." Her voice carried a layer of relief alongside a hint of defiance.

Ethan didn't like the idea, but there was no logical reason for her not to go home. The cops had been watching the place for days now, and before he left, Robert had searched her apartment for booby traps and surveillance, and had come up empty.

They'll be fine, he told himself, fighting to quell the buzz in his gut, the one that went along with the mental image of Nicole and Blake together, no matter the location.

He nodded stiffly. "That should be okay. Keep your eyes open, and call me if anything hinky happens. And I mean it," he stressed to the other man. *"Anything."*

"Then it's settled," Nicole said, voice cool. "I'm ready to leave when you are, Blake."

A gentleman to the bone, he escorted her

around the BMW and opened her door to usher her into the car's plush, leather-lined depths. Ethan glanced from the Beemer to the dusty, dented motorcycle and reminded himself that was the point. He was dented and barely functional. Blake was a damned luxury vehicle.

After closing Nicole's door, Blake walked around to the driver's side, pausing near Ethan. "You sure about this?"

Ethan nodded. "You guys will be fine."

"That wasn't what I meant."

"I know." Ethan wished the circumstances were different. Wished he were different. "Go on ahead. I'll lock up before I leave."

But he stood watching as the BMW eased down the drive, as the sound of its engine faded. Then, and only then, he allowed himself to kick at the gravel, a frustrated vent he hadn't wanted anyone else to see.

When that didn't make him feel the slightest bit better, he took a last check of Blake's cottage before locking up and setting the security system on a time delay that would give him a few minutes to get down the driveway. Then he climbed aboard the dented bike and pointed its nose back down the mountain, headed back to the Vault.

Alone.

WHEN ETHAN reached the main entrance to the Vault, he found that Clive's people had used some serious firepower to blast their way into the parking bay. One steel door hung askew, while the other lay crumpled off to the side. Chunks of cement were scattered everywhere he looked, and all that was left of the structure were the spiked remains of broken steel reinforcements.

The bad news was that the place was trashed. The good news was that it appeared deserted, with crime scene tape strung at regular intervals, indicating that Detective Riske or her local equivalent had come and gone.

Ethan felt a faint pinch of guilt for contaminating the crime scene as he ducked under the tape, but contented himself with the thought that they had Clive and his confession, and the cops had photos.

When he reached the parking garage, he cursed upon seeing that the half-dozen vehicles nearest the inner door were wrecked, their panels marred with bullet holes and scorch marks. He saw, though, that farther away from the blast site, his Jeep was relatively untouched. It was covered in a thick layer of gray dust and one tire looked as though it could use some air, but the vehicle should be able to make it out.

"At least something's going my way today," he muttered, leaning the dented bike against the concrete wall just inside the parking bay.

As he crossed to the Jeep, his cell phone rang, surprising him. He glanced around and saw that where there had been cement before, now there was sky, letting the cell signal through.

He flipped open the unit. "Ethan here."

"Ethan! Thank God." Evangeline's tone, the one she used when things were really going wrong on an op, tightened his gut.

"What's wrong?"

A burst of static drowned out her answer.

"Hang on," he said loudly, walking toward the blasted-out section to boost the signal. "Say again?"

"I said, we're pretty sure Clive isn't the mastermind of all the murders. There's someone else involved."

Ethan tightened his fingers on the phone, gripping it so tightly the plastic edges of the unit bit into his skin. "Who?"

"We don't know yet."

"Call Nicole," he said urgently. "She's with Blake Rothschild. Make sure they know they're in—"

A sharp blow slammed into the back of Ethan's head. He staggered forward and went down, fuzzily aware that the phone skittered away and was crushed beneath a booted foot. Nearly unconscious, he cursed and reached for his gun as the booted foot drew back and kicked him hard. The blow rolled him over just as a second kick caught him in the temple and knocked him out, with one panicked thought accompanying him into the blackness.

Nicole!

"GOD, I couldn't be happier to get into my own clothes," Nic said with a heartfelt groan as she jogged down the short flight of stairs to the lower floor of her safe, familiar one-bedroom apartment.

She found Blake in her kitchen, and was jarred by the sight of a man making sandwiches at her counter, and even more jarred by the faint jab of disappointment that his hair was sandy rather than gold-tipped brown, his clothes tailored rather than casually rugged.

When he turned and smiled at her, she instinctively lifted a hand to tug at her clothes, which somehow felt odd, as though so much had happened over the past few days that her body should have changed.

But she hadn't changed, and it was time to get back to her old life. Or rather, back to the new life she'd be making for the baby and herself.

She took a deep breath and told herself to smile, even though her stomach jangled. "You didn't need to cook."

Blake grinned. "I'm not sure sandwiches count as cooking, but given my past experience with needing my body guarded, I figured it'd been a while since you'd eaten on anything resembling a normal schedule."

"You can say that again," Nic said, and her laugh was genuine as she took a seat at the round table that was tucked into the open end of the kitchen.

She saw that he'd set two places and put

out coffee for himself, herbal tea for her. Her eyes wanted to fill when she realized he'd paid attention to what she'd asked for the first time they'd met, and had taken the trouble for her. Worse, the only thing it made her feel was uncomfortable.

When he set down her plate and his, then sat, she took a deep breath. "Listen, Blake. I don't know what or how much Ethan has told you about my situation, but…" She trailed off, not sure how to say what she thought needed to be said without sounding like an idiot if she'd misread the signals yet again.

"But you're in love with him," Blake finished for her.

"That wasn't what I was going to say." Nic did her best to hide a wince. "But, yeah. I'm in love with him."

Strangely enough, it felt good to say the words out loud, and realize that the world hadn't ended. Nothing fundamental had changed—or rather, it had changed days ago when she'd seen Ethan climbing down to rescue her from the elevator, or maybe months ago, when she'd first looked into his eyes and seen someone she wanted to know better.

Blake took her hand, linked their fingers and squeezed. "Don't stress. I'm offering you my friendship and funding for your project, nothing more."

Nic felt a hot blush stain her cheeks. "Oh." She lifted her hands to her face. "I'm sorry yet again. I know we talked about this before, but the way you were looking at me earlier, I thought—"

"You thought right, but no matter what Ethan told me about you being available, the look in his eye says otherwise. That look says *Hands off, she's mine.*"

"Or not." Nic sighed, but picked up her sandwich and dug in. "He can't handle the idea of family or responsibility, and I refuse to put myself down again by struggling to make things work with a man who doesn't love me enough to fight for me."

Blake frowned. "Don't you think—"

He was interrupted by a quiet knock at the front door, which was just down a short hall from the kitchen.

Ethan, Nic thought, her heart giving a sharp jolt at the thought he hadn't been able to bear the idea of her being alone with Blake.

She was halfway across the kitchen before

she was even aware of moving, only to have Blake catch her arm. "Wait," he said, voice low. "Let me get it, just in case."

Having experienced far too many unpleasant surprises over the past few days, Nic wasn't about to argue. She stayed close behind him as he headed for the door.

He was a step away when the panel exploded inward, kicked or rammed with such force the lock ripped away from the wooden door frame. The door slammed into Blake, sending him staggering back into Nic. He grabbed for her but missed, and she fell backward onto the floor as two men charged into the apartment.

One was tall and lean, his skin drawn so tight over his bones that it appeared shiny and faintly yellow. He wore a dark knit cap pulled low on his forehead and a navy jacket turned up at the collar, so that all she could see of his face was a hooked nose and a pair of cruel, ice-blue eyes. She recognized the other one instantly, recognized the blocky face, the straight nose and paradoxically full lips of the man from the hospital.

Panic slashed and she screamed when the first guy pulled a knife and lunged at Blake.

He dodged with a shout and grabbed for his attacker, twisting furiously in an effort to keep himself between Nic and both of the men. He ducked a punch, glanced back at her and snapped, "Run!"

Indecision froze her in place as Blake swung a vicious kick at one of the men. In the split second his guard came down, the other guy landed a crippling kidney-punch that sent Blake staggering. The guy from the hospital turned toward Nic, eyes glittering. "Come on, sweetheart. It'll go easier on you if you cooperate."

Nic spun and bolted away from the men, down a short hallway and through the kitchen, where a back door led to an alleyway behind the apartment building.

She slammed through the door and skidded into the alley, feeling the cold on her damp hair and through the thick wool of her socks. Turning for the main road, she let out a gasp of relief at the sight of a passing car and the blue bubble lights on its roof.

"Help!" she screamed, bolting for the police cruiser. "Help us!"

A man stepped out from behind a Dumpster just short of the main street. His features were shadowed, his silhouette broad and his fighting stance an immediate warning that flared panic into Nic's already panicked brain.

She skidded to a halt and cried out when something sliced through her sock and into her foot—glass or a piece of metal or something that cut into her flesh bringing a sick wash of pain. She spun and tried to run the other way, but she slipped on the slick blood and her consciousness swam with the pain. Staggering, she'd taken only two steps before the shadow closed in on her and the man grabbed her by the upper arm, his fingers digging into her flesh with punishing intensity.

Nic screamed and he twisted her arm behind her back and clamped his free hand across her mouth. Then he began dragging her deeper into the alley, toward where she saw a dark sedan parked behind an overly full Dumpster.

She struggled and clawed at him, but to no avail. The sedan's trunk popped open as they approached, and Nic screamed as he shoved her in and slammed the lid, cutting off the light.

She continued to scream as the engine came to life and car doors slammed. The noise echoed in the tiny, cramped space, hurting her ears and pounding the fear into her brain. She sobbed and clawed at the inner locking mechanism, which wouldn't budge, and howled when the car started moving, taking her away.

The jolting ride made her miserably sick within minutes, forcing her to curl up with her arms clamped across her belly. As she lay there with tears trickling down her face, she prayed for another chance, for rescue.

For Ethan.

Chapter Fourteen

When Robert drove them through the first set of blast doors and they saw the damage that had been done to the Vault, Evangeline's throat tightened. "Oh, no."

"Goddamn it." A muscle ticked at the corner of his jaw, and his fingers clutched the steering wheel, bloodless with the force of his grip. "Ethan is ours. We're not letting Clive and his thugs destroy anything else that belongs to us."

For the first time in a long, long time, since even before the plane crash, Evangeline believed it when he said "we" and "us," believed that it meant more than a marriage, something closer to a partnership. But though the new closeness she and Robert had found in Spain warmed her, worry for Ethan grew as Robert gunned the SUV down the short concrete tunnel and into the main parking garage.

"There!" Heart skipping a beat, she pointed to a corner of the lot, where the lights feeding off the backup generator left a darkly shadowed section.

"I see it." Jaw clenched, Robert sent them skidding into the corner, where they both jumped from the still-shuddering SUV to stare at a single hiking boot lying on the concrete.

Robert glanced at her. "Ethan's?"

"Yes," Evangeline whispered, throat tight. "But where—" She broke off at the muffled sound of another engine. "They're taking him somewhere!"

She spun back to their SUV, but stopped when Robert raised his hand. "Wait," he said. "It's not moving."

Sure enough, the engine noise didn't change in pitch or distance. The vehicle was idling. But where?

Evangeline drew the 9 mm she'd snagged from the safe house and followed the noise, conscious of her husband's warm, solid presence at her back.

They rounded a corner, where part of the ceiling had fallen in. Rocks and dirt littered the floor and the cement slabs made crazy angles that left Evangeline feeling tilted and unsteady, but the reinforcing metal beams were mostly in place, and the structure seemed solid enough. For the moment, anyway.

"I don't like the feel of this," Robert said under his breath.

"Me neither." But she kept going, passing a colossal chunk of concrete, and hesitating at the sight of something large and square hidden beneath a tent-sized blue tarp, which was weighted down with broken concrete.

The idling noise was coming from within.

"Ethan!" Evangeline bolted forward and yanked at the tarp. "Ethan, answer me!"

She heard nothing besides the engine's idle and the crinkle of the blue tarp, which fought her efforts to pull it free.

"Here. I've got it." Robert kicked away several of the cement weights and heaved, his muscles bunching with the effort as the tarp pulled aside to reveal Ethan's Jeep.

A gush of foul air washed into their faces, making Evangeline gag. "God. Ethan!"

The car windows were cracked at the top but so fogged that she couldn't see in. She fought her way across the sagging tarp and yanked at the driver's-side door, fearing the worst. She gasped when a heavy weight forced the door open and Ethan's limp body tumbled out.

She grabbed for him and nearly went down, saved only by her husband's strong grip around her waist, and by his hands steadying Ethan's dead weight. They lowered him carefully, then caught him beneath the arms and dragged him away from the foul air, around the corner to cleaner oxygen.

"Is he—?" She couldn't finish the question, fearing they had been too late, fearing that Clive and his associates had won, after all.

Robert felt for the other man's pulse and nodded. "He's breathing and his lips aren't blue. He must not've been in there too long, or else the tarp let in enough fresh air to keep him going." He pulled Ethan partway up to a sitting position and gave him a shake. "Hey, Moore, wake up! You sleeping on the job?"

Ethan groaned and muttered something that sounded anatomically impossible. Evangeline's lips curved. "I think he'll live."

Robert gave him another brusque shake. "Come on, Ethan. Nicole needs you."

That brought him around in an instant.

Ethan's eyes flew open and he reached up to grip Robert's wrists where the other man held his collar. "What happened?"

Robert shook his head. "We don't know all the details yet, but they went straight through Rothschild and snatched her from her place. Blake's in pretty rough shape, but he saw a dark green or dark blue sedan leaving, and wrote down plates that turned out to belong to a stolen HumVee, meaning they were switched out."

"In other words, you have no idea where she is." Ethan shook off Robert and struggled to his feet. He stood, swaying, as bloodlust flared in his eyes. "You have Fuentes?"

Robert nodded. "He's back at the safe house, but he's not talking yet."

"Take me there," Ethan ordered, his tone brooking no argument. "He'll talk to me."

ROBERT DROVE like a madman, but he still didn't go fast enough for Ethan. Through the stabbing headache brought on by carbon monoxide poisoning, one thought drummed over and over in his brain.

Nicole was counting on him. He couldn't let her down.

When they reached the safe house—an intentionally nondescript residence in a ruthlessly middle-class neighborhood outside Denver—he was the first one out of the car. His knees nearly buckled when he hit the ground running, but he forced himself to keep moving.

He didn't have time to be ill or injured. Not now. Not when Nic needed him most.

"Where is he?" Ethan demanded the moment he slammed through a side door into the kitchen, where Angel had set up shop at a butcher-block breakfast bar.

Instead of waving him past, the dark-clothed receptionist jumped up and stood in front of him, blocking his headlong rush.

A month ago—hell, even a few days ago—she would've ducked the question or gotten confused, or maybe pretended to. Now, hardened by danger and death, grown into the woman he suspected Evangeline had seen beneath her haphazard shell, Angel fisted her hands on her hips, barring him from entering the rest of the house as Robert and Evangeline came through the door behind him.

"Settle down," Angel ordered, her voice

surprisingly firm. "Take a breath and think about what you're doing. If you go in there half-cocked, Fuentes will know he has the upper hand from the get-go, and you'll come away with nothing. Is that what you want?"

Ethan took a deep breath because she was right, damn it. He needed to get a grip before he went any further, or else he risked losing everything.

He'd reacted without thinking once before, when he'd forsaken training to reach for Caro, and the burst of emotion had cost him. Now, he was damn well going to slow down and use his head, use all the logic he'd thought was his salvation but had turned out to be his excuse to keep himself separate from everyone else.

Well, he wasn't on his own now, Ethan knew. He was part of the team.

Sucking in a breath and then letting it out slowly, he said, "Okay." He took another breath and counted to three. "I'm cool."

Angel looked at him for a moment, then nodded. "Yeah. I think you are." She stepped aside. "He's in the second bedroom on the left. Cam and John are in there with him, but they haven't gotten anything new. He just keeps repeating that this was all because of Robert."

Evangeline's husband muttered a curse, but at the moment, Ethan didn't really care why, he only cared about getting Clive to tell him where Nicole had been taken. She was all that mattered right now.

By the time Ethan opened the door to the back bedroom, he had tamped his panic down to cold, logical rage. Inside the small room, the bed had been shoved up against a wall to clear the center of the room. There, Clive sat in a heavy chair, cuffed to the sturdy wood by his wrists and ankles. Wearing a stained and rumpled suit, he still managed to exude the graceful power Ethan had noted in the photographs PPS had managed to collect.

Cold logic, he reminded himself when the rage threatened to swamp him. Brutal self-control kept him from flinging himself on Fuentes and strangling the bastard. Instead, he jerked his chin at Cam and John, who sat in folding chairs against the opposite wall, keeping watch over the prisoner. "Give us a minute, will you?"

The other men rose. John leaned down to glare at Clive, lips pulled back in a sneer.

"We'll be back." Then he left, with Cam following.

As they passed, Cam gripped Ethan's shoulder briefly in a gesture that transmitted support and respect, and a level of friendship Ethan wasn't sure he deserved, but was damn sure going to try to earn in the next few minutes.

When the others were gone and the door had shut in their wake, Ethan grabbed one of the unoccupied chairs and spun it around so he could straddle it and lean his folded arms on the backrest as he glared at the captured but unbowed ex-spy.

Ethan wasn't a trained interrogator, and as far as he knew, they were fresh out of truth serum and torture devices. Among the PPS operatives, Robert probably had the most experience with this sort of thing, along with a hell of a motivation, yet he'd been unable to crack Fuentes's silence, which boded ill for this interrogation.

But Ethan figured he had one slim advantage over his compatriots—lack of emotional involvement with Fuentes.

He was involved with Nic, true—involved right up to his eyeballs—but Fuentes had meant nothing to him until he'd messed with Nicole.

Logic, he told himself. *Use your brain, damn it.*

Something had always bugged him about the progression of attacks against PPS. Now, he sat across from the man who was supposed to have masterminded everything, including Robert's crash two years earlier, the murders of Nick Warner and the others, and the attacks on the Denver office building and the Vault. And sitting there, he knew deep down inside that it didn't play. It wasn't rational.

It made sense that Fuentes had tried to kill Robert to protect the illicit deals he'd been running through PPS years earlier, but that had been a business decision.

Now, fighting the urge to throttle the man who held Nicole's safety in his hands, Ethan said, "You don't hate Robert."

Fuentes didn't react except to narrow his eyes. "Am I supposed to agree, or are you going to tell me the answers to your questions even before you ask them? That's an interesting interrogation technique, Mr. Moore. One they taught you in the military, perhaps?

Along with those advanced lifesaving skills that stood you in such good stead with your wife?"

Ethan told himself to ignore the cruel barb. After a moment, he continued. "The plane crash was a necessity because Robert had gotten too close to your business and you needed him out of the way. Nick Warner died because he was going to squeal on your investment scheme. Maybe the murder of the other investors was your idea, too. They were loose ends to be tied up, leaving more of the profit for you."

Ethan paused, gauging the other man's reactions, which were hidden too well behind a professional's mask. He continued, "But the other attacks—Lenny's death, the office building bombing, the man who went after Nicole—those weren't business. They were terrorism, and I don't think you're a terrorist."

The prisoner lifted his chin almost imperceptibly, but Ethan caught the motion. Clive was a businessman, logical and unemotional, whereas these latest attacks had been almost pure emotion, driven by hatred of PPS or its founders.

At the thought, a connection chimed in his brain. Clive had said the attacks were all because of Robert. All because someone hated Robert enough to kill. But who?

He stood, opened the door partway and stuck his head out into the hallway, which was jammed with PPS staff. "I need Robert in here."

When Evangeline followed her husband, Ethan didn't say anything. He knew better than to argue with his boss when she had that look in her eye.

Once the door was closed again, Ethan looked from Robert to Clive and back again. Behind well-trained facades, he saw rage and regret, guilt and hubris, but he didn't see hatred.

He turned to Robert. "Who hates you?"

The fact that the other man didn't react to the question suggested that Ethan wasn't the only one trying to think this through logically.

After a moment's pause, Robert answered, "My enemy list includes any number of people whose lives changed because of my actions back in MI6, along with a handful of governments and several large corporations."

He shook his head. "But none of those possibilities feel right."

In addition, none of them had garnered the
slightest reaction from Fuentes, Ethan
noticed, though he wasn't sure if that was a
clue or a result of the other man's training.

"It feels more personal," Robert continued. "But I can't think of anyone who'd hate
me that way. Not enough to kill over,
anyway."

"Which is the sticking point," Evangeline
agreed. "We're not just looking for someone
who hates Robert, we're looking for
someone vicious and ruthless enough not to
care about collateral damage."

"Or someone self-centered—or angry—
enough to think that the end justifies the
means," Ethan said. He rose and began to
pace the length of the small, crowded
bedroom, needing an outlet for the restless
energy that buzzed beneath his skin at the
knowledge that each passing minute in-
creased Nic's danger. "Someone even a little
bit unbalanced, a little bit—" He broke off
as the door opened and Angel stuck her head
through, then handed Robert a note.

Ethan crowded close to Evangeline so they

could watch him unfold the single-page computer printout, which appeared to be a record of company ownership. It took him a moment to backtrack the legalese, but when he did, he cursed under his breath.

The Rocky Mountain Sky helicopter tour company was owned by an O. Turner. The same O. Turner who had authorized the sale of the decommissioned MI-8 to Rocky Mountain Sky in an effort to get the chopper off the TCM books and hide its ownership.

"Olivia." Ethan spoke the name on a hiss of indrawn breath.

Even before he saw the confirmation spark in Clive's eyes, he knew they had their name. It made a twisted sort of sense once he knew to look for the connections: she was the wife of TCM's owner, Stephen Turner, and the mother of Peter Turner, who was one of the major conspirators already uncovered during the PPS investigation. More importantly in terms of the recent attacks, she was Robert's ex-wife, which, depending on a history that Ethan knew nothing about, might give her reason—at least in her mind—to hate him.

"But she's nuts," Evangeline protested. "That's why we crossed her off the suspect list. Remember how Kyle said she acted at Stephen's birthday party? She's seriously un-balanced. There's no way she could've set up the shell corporation that hid the investment scheme, or even pulled off those murders."

"But Peter could have," Ethan responded. He watched Clive out of the corner of his eye, wishing he knew more about body language. "And after Peter was injured and went into a coma, she could have turned to Clive." Now he faced the shackled man. "What I don't get is why he hooked up with a woman like that. Was it sex? Power? A little bit of both?"

Clive turned his head away and didn't answer.

Ethan felt the minutes ticking away beneath his skin. He wanted to be out of there, chasing Olivia, but what was the use? Until they had a starting point for their search, his time was better spent here.

"Olivia. Damn." Robert had gone a strange shade of gray. "I knew she hadn't take the divorce well, but she seemed okay with Stephen." He glared at Fuentes. "You pushed her, didn't you? She was never as strong as us, and you knew it. You just kept at her until she broke. Until—" He snapped his teeth shut on the words, which were no help to them now, only hissing under his breath, *"Bastard."*

Come on, Ethan thought, paying only half his attention to Robert. *Come on, think!* Clive wasn't giving anything away, so it was up to them to figure out the connections.

What had brought Olivia and Clive together in the first place? Power, Ethan figured. Money. Oil rights. If Olivia—

He froze mid-pace, his mind locking on the word. *Oil.* Olivia had used her current husband's company to hide behind when she, Peter and Clive had concocted the shell companies to buy up all the oil rights near the Ward ranch by fair means or foul. She was focused—obsessed, even—by the money, power and prestige she believed the oil money would bring her.

Which was why the attacks had seemed personal, not just on Robert, but on Nicole, as well.

"I think I know where they are," Ethan announced, and took off at a dead run, hoping to hell he wouldn't be too late to save her.

Chapter Fifteen

Bruised and battered and sick to her stomach, Nic moaned when the vehicle rolled to a halt and the engine stopped with a shuddering cough that let in the sound of raindrops on the trunk lid.

She tightened her arms across her stomach, praying the nausea was simple car sickness and not something far worse. *Please, let the baby be safe,* she thought fervently. *Please let us get out of this alive.*

Then she heard footsteps on wet pavement, and panic blotted out even those prayers. Panic and the drumming need to live, to fight, to do something other than lie still and wait. That was the old Nicole's way of life. She was the new Nicole now. She was a mother. A fighter.

Telling herself it was now or never, Nic rolled onto her queasy stomach and braced her arms and legs on the scratchy carpeting that covered the floor of the trunk. The footsteps stopped very near her and the trunk lid popped open.

Now! She erupted, screaming as she launched herself up and off to one side, lashing one numb leg in a roundhouse kick.

Her foot connected, and the guy from the hospital staggered back two steps, clutching his gut. Behind him, she saw a parking lot and trees. Freedom!

Breath sobbing in her lungs, she scrambled to her feet and ran, weaving drunkenly on numb legs and sock-clad feet, pushing her body as hard and as fast as she possibly could. She was screaming aloud, screaming in her head, her only goal to get away. Moments later, dull shock rattled through her when she recognized her surroundings. They were at a school—at *her* school, in the back parking lot of Donner High, near the soccer field and the little greenhouse and lab she'd used grant money to build.

Her steps faltered. Why had they brought her here? What possible reason—

A man's weight hit her from behind, sending her to her knees on the tarmac. She cried out in shock and pain as the pavement ground through her clothes and scraped at her knees and elbows. Her captor's heavy weight pressed her into the hard surface, cutting off her breath and trapping the screams in her lungs.

"Nice try, Miss Benedict." The taller, leaner man's voice was disturbingly polite, his hands almost gentle as he shifted his weight, slapped a strip of adhesive across her mouth, and then bound her wrists behind her back with the quick, efficient "snick" of a zip tie. "Unfortunately for you, you're not that fast. Which is fortunate for me, because my employer doesn't take kindly to failure and Leo and I—" he indicated the guy from the hospital with a jerk of his head "—have already had a few problems bringing you in. This was, so to speak, our last chance."

He climbed to his feet and dragged her upright. Nic twisted and fought, shouting behind her gag, but he had the advantage of leverage and size, and barely seemed to notice her struggles as he started walking the way she'd come—away from the school and the main road, back toward the soccer field and her greenhouse.

Nic's mind nearly blanked with panic, with despair, but she forced herself to fight through the layers of weakness and hold it together. Ethan would come for her. She had to believe that, even though it might not be logical.

Screw logic—she believed in him. He didn't love her, but he'd vowed to protect her. Once he found out they'd hurt Blake and taken her, he'd never rest until he found her.

The possibility that he might be too late weighed on her, bringing tears to her eyes as her captor, now joined by the man he'd called Leo, shoved her through the greenhouse door into the warm, humid interior.

She'd closed the greenhouse and lab at the end of the school year and had done regular drive-bys. Two weeks earlier, the place had been locked up tight. Now the locks were broken, and one of the tarps she'd used to cover the planting area was gone. A fire pit had been dug in the soil and garbage lay piled nearby, a mishmash of potato chip bags and empties, with a pair of folding chairs abandoned off to one side.

The sight brought a prickle of tears. Even more than her apartment, the greenhouse was Nic's sanctuary, the one thing she could point to and say *that's mine*. She'd conceived the project, organized the start-up funding and persuaded the Donner High administrative board to let her use a piece of their prized soccer field. It was hers.

Though the damage was fixable, it was an invasion. The final insult in a week full of them, which brought a spurt of anger to chase away the tears.

Nic began to struggle anew, and cursed the men from behind her gag as Leo grabbed her by the hair and shoved her through an open door at the back of the greenhouse, and into the lab itself. She cried out and stumbled forward, and with her hands bound behind her back, she couldn't stop herself from slamming into the converter, an oversized still she and her students used to ferment corn and other plants into ethanol-based fuel.

Gasping with pain, she leaned back against the converter and looked around the lab.

She'd packed away most of the equipment for the summer, leaving eight stone-topped lab benches, the converter and a row of locked cabinets, making the space look

like the modern update of an ancient sacri-
ficial chamber, a skewed perception that
was only reinforced when a woman
appeared in the doorway.

She was shorter than Nic, her dark, curly
hair styled with pricey elegance, and though
her skin was unlined, her conservative
clothes put her in her fifties. She was the
very picture of a country club wife until Nic
got to her eyes, which were emerald-green
and devoid of emotion.

And, Nic realized with sharp panic, she
was also a complete stranger.

"Why?" she said, forgetting the gag, which
made the word come out as a muffled
syllable.

The woman seemed to understand,
though. She bared her teeth. "Because you're
out to get me. You're all out to get me. Robert
left me and married that FBI bitch, and now
they're both after my land. And you." Her expression twisted to something cruel and an-
ticipatory. "You with your biofuel. You think
I don't know what you're planning? Well, it
won't work. Oil will always equal money
and power."

Nic stared in disbelief. The converter was

a scaled-up and slightly modified version of a basic design that'd been in use for decades. "You're insane," she mumbled behind the gag. "This is nothing more than an overgrown science project."

"They've always called visionaries crazy, haven't they?" The woman yanked the adhesive off Nic's mouth and her face split in a wide, predatory grin. "They'll see in the end. They'll see that I was right, that I was powerful—more powerful than Robert and his little tramp wife, more powerful than Stephen, who loves the company more than he loves me. More powerful even than Clive, who thought he was using me when all along I was the one using him."

Through the insanity, the woman had started to sound all too sane, Nic realized as her captor's eyes cooled from manic to icy logic, which was far more dangerous. She nodded to Leo, who'd taken up a position at the doorway. "Is everything set?"

"Yes, ma'am."

The woman nodded. "Then strap her down and let's get the hell out of here."

The taller man dragged Nic toward the converter and around to the far side of the squat unit. There, she saw something that shouldn't have been there—a flat, square box with wires sprouting from the top and winding to a second, smaller square. A short antenna protruded from the top of the second box, and the whole thing was fixed to the side of the biofuel converter by a pair of nylon cargo straps. *A bomb!*

Nic didn't realize she'd screamed until the woman stepped very close to her, leaned in and smiled. "Just between us girls, it's so much more elegant than a rocket launcher, don't you think?"

As if a light switch had been thrown, illuminating a dim room, Nic remembered everything. She could see the dark helicopter in her mind's eye, could pick out all of the details she'd been unable to remember before. She saw how the pilot had looked away right before impact. She saw how the figure on the helicopter skids had pumped his fist once the rocket took flight. And she saw, quite clearly, the passenger sitting beside the pilot. It hadn't been an indistinct figure after all. It had been a woman. This woman.

"You're Olivia Turner," she said, making the connection.

The woman preened. "You've heard of me."

"Don't do this," Nic said. "Please. I've never done anything to you. And..." She faltered. "I'm pregnant."

Olivia stared at her for a long moment with those cold, dead eyes, before gesturing for the men to proceed. "Do it."

"Hold her," Leo ordered. Sweating lightly in the warmth that spilled in from the greenhouse, he brought out a second set of cargo straps. While the leaner guy held Nic, bracing against her furious struggles, Leo fastened one of the straps to her right ankle, then looped the binding around one of the solid steel struts of the reactor.

Nic whimpered, knowing that those struts were bolted into an equally thick steel plate, attaching the converter to the floor of the prefab laboratory building.

"A fitting end, don't you think?" the woman asked conversationally. "If you'd just left well enough alone, it never would have come to this."

How? Nic thought desperately. She hadn't done anything to this woman, hadn't done anything except try to make a life for herself, a family for herself. She hadn't done anything!

Exactly, that little voice whispered inside. You *never* do *anything.*

Olivia glanced at her watch and smiled slightly.

"No doubt Clive has squealed by now, so your lover-boy should be on his way. Feel free to scream for him. Knowing those too-loyal idiots who work for Robert, most of PPS will be on his heels. With any luck, you'll take the whole lot of them with you when this place goes up." Her smile widened. "And just to make it more interesting…" She beckoned to Leo, who handed her a small, snub-nosed revolver.

She lifted the weapon, aimed it at Nic, and fired.

Nic screamed as her world went red. Shock and pain dropped her to her knees and she thrashed as the zip ties prevented her from grabbing her right shoulder. Agony erupted in her opposite shoulder, suggesting that the bullet had ricocheted off the converter to strike her a second time.

Hot red wetness seeped through Nic's shirt. The first wash of pain faded slightly, leaving her numb and cold and so weak she could barely hold herself in a sitting position, with her back braced against the converter.

Emerald eyes glittering with satisfaction, Olivia returned the weapon to Leo. "You hid the truck in the forest, on that access road, right?"

"Yes, ma'am."

Seeming satisfied, she waved them out. "Let's go." Before the door swung shut at her back, she turned back to Nic once more. "Sorry there's no countdown display on the device, so you'll have to do the math in your head." She lifted a small transmitter. "You'll hear a click when I hit the remote. After the click you've got three minutes to live. Enjoy them."

When the door swung shut behind her and the sound of their footsteps receded in the distance, Nic slumped to the floor, curling to lie on her side with tears streaming down her face. "I'm sorry," she whispered to the baby growing inside her. "I'm so sorry."

ETHAN TURNED Robert's SUV into the parking lot of Donner High School on two wheels, cursing when he found the parking lot empty. He hit the gas and sent the vehicle flying around the school at nearly sixty mph, then stood on the brakes, heart locking in his throat when he saw the dark blue sedan Blake had described, sitting at the far end of the lot.

Beyond it sat a neat greenhouse and a prefab steel shed. Nicole's lab.

He sent the SUV hurtling past the sedan. The tires slid on the wet grass, chewing up the turf when he hit the brakes and slapped the vehicle into Park, but he didn't care. He only cared about capturing Olivia and rescuing Nicole.

This would end now.

He hit the ground running. He was nearly to the greenhouse when he saw movement in the forest beyond—Olivia was slipping out the back with two of her men. A quick scan of the parking lot showed that the others were just arriving, with Robert and Evangeline leading the way in a borrowed truck.

They weren't nearly close enough. Olivia was going to escape if he didn't go after her.

The inner battle was brief and fierce, and Ethan's feet were moving even before he was conscious of having made the decision, but it was the logical one. None of them would be safe if Olivia got away.

As he pounded in pursuit, he yanked the 9 mm from his waistband. Another man might have fired a warning shot. Ethan aimed for flesh.

The taller man screamed and went down, writhing and clutching his left leg. Rather than stopping or turning to fight, Olivia and the other guy put their heads down and ran faster, headed deeper into the forest.

Ethan's second shot missed, the bullet embedding itself in a tree trunk. Cursing, he ran into the forest. A blur erupted from his left and the second man hit him in a flying tackle. The men went down in a tangle of arms and legs, fighting and cursing, punching and tearing at each other.

Rage hazed Ethan's vision, but he was aware that Olivia paused for a moment nearby, then slipped into the woods. She was getting away!

Refusing to let that happen, he drove his fist into the other guy's jaw in a powerful knockout blow. Leaving the unconscious thug lying in the pine litter, he struggled to his feet and ran after Olivia.

He hadn't gone twenty feet when a gunshot ripped through the air and a burning impact slammed into his upper arm. Ethan shouted and spun toward the sound of the shot, then ducked as Olivia fired the small .22 again.

The round jammed and the blowback singed her hand, making her screech in pain. Taking advantage of that split-second opportunity, Ethan ducked and lunged at her, grabbing her around the waist and sending them crashing to the ground.

His ingrained reluctance to hurt a woman had him struggling to subdue her while keeping the .22 pointed safely away. He earned an elbow in the teeth for his effort. Tasting blood, he cursed, rolled over and leaned his full weight on her, trapping her beneath him. With one hand holding her gun wrist, he got his other arm across her throat and bore down until she gurgled for breath.

Their positions put them face-to-face and left him staring into her emerald-green eyes, which gleamed with fury and madness. "Let me go!" she hissed with what little breath he'd allowed her, and her eyes went calculating. "Let me go and I'll tell you how to save her."

The words punched through the bloodred

haze of fighting madness that had overtaken him. Nicole!

He leaned on her throat until her eyes bulged. "Tell me or you're dead."

And damned if he didn't mean it. To hell with not hurting women. She wasn't a woman to him anymore. She was a murderer, and she held Nicole's future in her hands.

Olivia squirmed beneath him, her slight body seeming too insubstantial to have done the things she'd done. When he didn't ease up, she whispered, "In my pocket."

Ethan heard the others approaching through the woods and knew Robert would be there any moment, looking to take over. He'd try to do the right thing, but he had his own priorities, whereas Ethan had only one: to save Nicole.

He twisted Olivia's wrist sharply until the .22 fell free, then shifted his weight to free her other hand. "No garbage, I'm warning you."

She shook her head slightly, fear and resignation dominating in her eyes as she reached inside her coat and withdrew a remote control of some sort.

A lightning bolt of panic split Ethan as he

realized he'd horribly, brutally miscalculated. He bore down on Olivia's neck and twisted, grabbing for the remote.

By the time he'd wrestled it away from her, the red indicator light at the top of the unit was blinking to indicate that a countdown had begun.

"Better hurry," Olivia whispered, eyes beginning to dull. "You've got three minutes."

NIC'S WORLD had gone gray, but she roused partway when she heard the click that signaled the bomb's arming.

She was vaguely aware of being curled on the floor of her lab, but the cement floor didn't feel cold anymore. It was warm and fuzzy. Everything was warm and fuzzy, even the pain in her upper arm and opposite shoulder.

She was dying, she knew. She and the baby both, and for what? Because she'd been in the wrong place at the wrong time, and because she'd fallen in love with the wrong man. It was all so bloody unfair that she wanted to scream, but she didn't have the energy, so she let her eyelids drift shut and counted her heartbeats.

Her last thoughts were of a hummed

lullaby and a whispered apology to a child who would never be born.

THE MOMENT Ethan stepped into the small prefab room beyond the ruined greenhouse, he was thrust back into his worst nightmare.

Nicole lay horribly still, eyes closed. Her hands were bound behind her back and her front was painted red with the blood that pooled beneath her. Ethan whispered her name, dropped to his knees and reached out to touch her.

In an instant, he was back on the streets of Vegas, reaching for the woman he'd loved. Pulling her toward him. Killing her.

He froze without touching her. *Wait,* he thought. *Think it through. Don't move her until you're sure.* It looked like a bullet wound, probably from Olivia's .22. If the bullet was still inside and he moved her the wrong way, he could cause more damage. He needed time to properly assess her wounds, or better yet, wait for the real paramedics.

Then he looked up and saw a deadly device strapped to the side of the big machine, saw a red light atop it blinking down the seconds.

They didn't *have* time.

Cursing, he reached to undo the cargo strap binding her ankle. He didn't know enough about bombs to guess whether he could unstrap it safely. Knowing Olivia's love for collateral damage, he doubted it, which made escape his only option.

"Nic, honey." He touched her neck and found that her pulse was dangerously slow, her breathing dangerously shallow. She couldn't stand to lose any more blood, but she couldn't stay where she was. They were probably down to a minute on Olivia's three-minute countdown, he thought as he pulled off his shirt and used it to form a crude pressure bandage, held in place with his belt.

She was dead either way, he told himself, reaching down to touch her cool lips with his.

"Ethan."

He jolted at her whisper, at the feel of her lips moving against his. He didn't dare touch her, didn't dare gather her close when she shifted toward him. Instead he pressed a hand to her shoulder where the blood had started anew at her motion. "Lie still. I'm—"

He broke off. He was what? Going to sit

there until they died together, along with their unborn child? That would be letting Olivia win. That would be letting the fear win.

He took a deep breath and looked down to find Nic staring at him with absolute faith and trust in her violet eyes. Her lips shaped two words. *Do it.* Then six more. *I trust you. I love you.*

Instead of added panic, the words found an answering chord within him, a spiraling sense of power, of faith.

He leaned forward and touched his lips to hers. "I love you, too. I'll show you just how much as soon as I get you out of here."

He slid his arms behind her shoulders and knees, cupping her body against his chest. Then, knowing he was taking the biggest, most important risk of his life, he stood, lifting her.

She gave a small, pained cry and her lips went white. Blood seeped beneath the pressure bandage to stain his chest, and he could feel his own heart drumming nearly through his skin, as though its strong beat could keep hers going.

He pressed his cheek against the top of

her head, held her tight and turned for the door. "Hang on, Nic. I've got you, but we need to move fast."

Even as he said that, the bomb gave off a loud click, and a high, subsonic whine began to build.

Praying as he'd never prayed before, Ethan ran, his arms full of the most important thing in his life.

His family.

He bolted through the greenhouse, wincing at every jolt. He was pretty sure Nic had passed out, and shifted his grip to press down on her shoulder, trying to keep the blood inside, where she needed it to keep her brain oxygenated.

The whine grew louder behind him and he heard shouting up ahead. He burst from the greenhouse and met a handful of PPS operatives headed in.

"Out!" he shouted. "It's wired to blow!"

Robert tried to take Nicole, but Ethan held him away. "I've got her. She needs an ambulance." The words were ragged in his throat, his breath labored in his lungs as he and the rest of the team ran across the field, headed away from the greenhouse as fast as—

The blast knocked him forward, roaring

over him like a thousand jet engines firing at once. He braced himself and rolled with the fall, protecting Nic as best he could. Moments later, a heavy weight landed atop him, then another. It took him a second to realize his teammates had offered up their own bodies as shields as shrapnel rained down on them.

When the noise, flame and fury had subsided, the others moved away. Fearing what he would find, Ethan eased away and looked down at Nic.

Her skin was bloodlessly pale, but her eyes were open and clear, and as he watched, her lips moved, shaping the words, *I love you.*

Heart suddenly so full it was nearly bursting, Ethan leaned down to whisper, as the sirens of approaching ambulances rose in the near distance, "Then I guess that means you'll have to marry me."

MARRY ME. As Nic floated back up through the warm layers of consciousness, she imagined she heard those words echoing in Ethan's voice. It seemed like an impossible dream, but part of her was sure he'd really done it, really asked her to marry him.

That should've been impossible. Then again, it should've been impossible for her to survive Olivia's mad plan, and she'd done that, hadn't she?

The beep of a monitor and the antiseptic smell of hospital told her she'd survived, all right. Even better, a second, faster beep beneath the first confirmed what she already knew in her heart, that the baby was doing fine despite everything.

Our baby's a survivor, she thought with an inner smile, *just like her parents.*

She wasn't sure how she knew it was a girl, but she did. A little girl with her mother's hair and sense of adventure, with her father's gorgeous eyes and ability to use logic when it suited, much to her parents' endless amusement and dismay.

The thought of it, the certainty of it, widened Nic's smile.

"What's going on in that head of yours? You telling yourself a joke?"

Nic opened her eyes and turned toward the sound of Ethan's voice. Squinting into the light, she was able to make out his stern features, was able to see the strain at the corners of his eyes, and the warmth of love within.

"No joke," she whispered, wincing from the pull of soreness in her throat at the tug of stitches from where the doctors had gone in to repair a torn lung on one side, a shattered scapula on the other. "Just thinking about the future."

When he just stood there for a half second, she caught her breath, suddenly fearing it'd been a dream, after all. Then he smiled, and in his eyes she saw all the love and reassurance she'd been looking for, all the futures she could ever want.

"I hope you saw me in it." He leaned over her and touched his lips to hers. "I hope you saw the three of us together, and maybe one or two more little rug rats so our kids will never be lonely at night, and they'll always have someone to turn to when things get tough."

"That—" Nic broke off when a big ball of happy tears lodged in her throat. "That sounds perfect."

There was movement behind Ethan, and she turned to watch as first one, then six, then at least twenty people crowded into her hospital room. She recognized Robert and Evangeline, wrapped together as though they planned to stay that way for a very long time. Angel was there, black clothing and makeup still firmly in place, but with a new softness to her expression. Blake stood near the back, sporting a black eye and stitches high on one cheek but when her eyes lit on him, he flashed her a thumbs-up.

Nic didn't recognize the others, but Ethan introduced them one by one. The smooth-looking charmer with light brown hair and a tan was ex-Ranger PPS operative Jack Sanders and the pretty, friendly-looking blonde beside him was his former protectee, Kelly Warner, whose husband had been killed in the first step of Olivia's plan. The dark, handsome hunk beside them was ex-cop PPS operative Mike Lawson, who was paired with lovely, auburn-haired Cassie Allen, a computer whiz Nic thought she'd met before, possibly in the Vault. The taller, younger man with piercing green eyes was Cameron Morgan, another former Ranger-turned-operative, who held hands with Jennie Ward, a tall, golden woman who reminded Nic of open spaces and the outdoors. Kyle Prescott was a younger version of his father, Robert, with darker hair but the same eyes and air of authority, though he looked a bit shell-shocked, suggesting that he was still dealing with learning of his mother's crimes. Beside him stood ex-FBI PPS operative Sara Montgomery, a striking dark-haired woman who only had eyes for Kyle. Rounding out the group was Navajo sharpshooter John Pinto and rookie agent Lily Clark.

Each and every one of them sported a puff of gauze taped at the crook of his or her arm.

Ethan shifted to sit on the edge of Nic's bed and took her hand in his. As he did so, she saw that he, too, had a bandage at his elbow. He followed her gaze, smiled and tightened his fingers on hers. "Everyone donated blood. Some of it went to you and the rest went into the blood bank."

"No." She shook her head. "It all went to me, to us." She smiled at the tough guys of PPS, and at the women who loved them. "Guess that makes us family, huh?"

Evangeline nodded and pressed closer to her husband, looking up at him with a flirtatious gleam in her eyes. "One big, happy, semi-functional family. That's us. At least it will be once we rebuild the offices and relocate the Vault, now that Clive, Olivia and the others are safely behind bars." She cut her eyes to Ethan. "You're staying, right? No more of this freelancing garbage. We can build you an actual office with your name on the door, right?"

"I need to talk to my fiancée about it," Ethan said, lifting Nic's hand and kissing her knuckles. "But if I get the okay, then yeah, you can build me an office. I might even take a repeat customer now and then, as long as I can make it home every night."

A ghost of a smile touched Robert's lips. "I think that can be arranged. I think it can all be arranged."

And deep down inside, Nic knew it would be. There would be some bumps along the way, but that was life, and the sum total of it all would be so much more than she'd had before, so much more than she'd ever imagined having. She had Ethan now, and in six more months or so, they'd have their daughter to complete the circle: a little girl they'd name Caroline. She'd grow up with the kids of all the couples crowding the hospital room, and they'd all get together for big, noisy dinners in their big, noisy houses, and it would be just like the family Nic had always dreamed of, only so much better, because PPS wasn't just a group of coworkers.

They were a team.

* * * * *

Look for Jessica Andersen's next book of romantic suspense in September 2007 when she concludes Harlequin Intrigue's LIGHTS OUT *continuity with* MEET ME AT MIDNIGHT.

Welcome to cowboy country...

Turn the page for a sneak preview of
TEXAS BABY
by
Kathleen O'Brien
An exciting new title from
Harlequin Superromance for everyone
who loves stories about the West

Harlequin Superromance—
Where life and love weave together
in emotional and unforgettable ways

CHAPTER ONE

CHASE TRANSFERRED his gaze to the road and identified a foreign spot on the horizon. A car. Almost half a mile away, where the straight, tree-lined drive met the public road. He could tell it was coming too fast, but judging the speed of a vehicle moving straight toward you was tricky.

It wasn't until it was about two hundred yards away that he realized the driver must be drunk…or crazy. Or both.

The guy was going maybe sixty. On a private drive, out here in ranch country, where kids or horses or tractors or stupid chickens might come darting out any minute, that was criminal. Chase straightened from his comfortable slouch and waved his hands.

"Slow down, you fool," he called out. He

took the porch steps quickly and began walking fast down the driveway.

The car veered oddly, from one lane to another, then up onto the slight rise of the thick green spring grass. It just barely missed the fence.

"Slow down, damn it!"

He couldn't see the driver, and he didn't recognize this automobile. It was small and old, and couldn't have cost much even when it was new. It was probably white, but now it needed either a wash or a new paint job or both.

"Damn it, what's wrong with you?"

At the last minute, he had to jump away, because the idiot behind the wheel clearly wasn't going to turn to avoid a collision. He couldn't believe it. The car kept coming, finally slowing a little, but it was too late.

Still going about thirty miles an hour, it slammed into the large, white-brick pillar that marked the front boundaries of the house. The pillar wasn't going to give an inch, so the car had to. The front end folded up like a paper fan.

It seemed to take forever for the car to settle, as if the trauma happened in slow motion, reverberating from the front to the back of the car in ripples of destruction. The front windshield suddenly seemed to ice over with lethal bits of glassy frost. Then the side windows exploded.

The front driver's door wrenched open, as if the car wanted to expel its contents. Metal buckled hideously. Small pieces, like hubcaps and mirrors, skipped and ricocheted insanely across the oyster-shell driveway.

Finally, everything was still. Into the silence, a plume of steam shot up like a geyser, smelling of rust and heat. Its snake-like hiss almost smothered the low, agonized moan of the driver.

Chase's anger had disappeared. He didn't feel anything but a dull sense of disbelief. Things like this didn't happen in real life. Not in his life. Maybe the sun had actually put him to sleep....

But he was already kneeling beside the car. The driver was a woman. The frosty glass-ice of the windshield was dotted with small flecks of blood. She must have hit it with her head, because just below her hairline a red liquid was seeping out. He touched it. He tried to wipe it away before it reached her eyebrow, though, of course that made no sense at all. Her eyes were shut.

Was she conscious? Did he dare move her? Her dress was covered in glass, and the metal of the car was sticking out lethally in all the wrong places.

Then he remembered, with an intense relief, that every good medical man in the county was here, just behind the house, drinking his champagne. He found his phone and paged Trent.

The woman moaned again.

Alive, then. Thank God for that.

He saw Trent coming toward him, starting out at a lope, but quickly switching to a full run.

"Get Dr. Marchant," Chase called. "Don't bother with 911."

Trent didn't take long to assess the situation. A fraction of a second, and he began pulling out his cell phone and running toward the house.

The yelling seemed to have roused the woman. She opened her eyes. They were blue and clouded with pain and confusion.

"Chase," she said.

His breath stalled. His head pulled back. "What?"

Her only answer was another moan, and he wondered if he had imagined the word. He reached around her and put his arm behind her shoulders. She was tiny. Probably petite by nature, but surely way too thin. He could feel her shoulder blades pushing against her skin, as fragile as the wishbone in a turkey.

She seemed to have passed out, so he put his other arm under her knees and lifted her out. He tried to avoid the jagged metal, but her skirt caught on a piece and the tearing sound seemed to wake her again.

"No," she said. "Please."

"I'm just trying to help," he said. "It's going to be all right."

She seemed profoundly distressed. She wriggled in his arms, and she was so weak, like a broken bird. It made him feel too big and brutish. And intrusive. As if touching her this way, his bare hands against the warm skin behind her knees, were somehow a transgression.

He wished he could be more delicate. But he smelled gasoline, and he knew it wasn't safe to leave her here.

Finally he heard the sound of voices, as guests began to run around the side of the house, alerted by Trent. Dr. Marchant was at the front, racing toward them as if he were forty instead of seventy. Susannah was right behind him, her green dress floating around her trim legs.

"Please," the woman in his arms murmured again. She looked at him, the expression in her blue eyes lost and bewildered. He wondered if she might be on drugs. Hitting her head on the windshield might account for this unfocused, glazed look, but it couldn't explain the crazy driving.

"Please, put me down. Susannah… The wedding…"

Chase's arms tightened instinctively, and he froze in his tracks. She whimpered, and he realized he might be hurting her. "Say that again?"

"The wedding. I have to stop it."

* * * * *

*Be sure to look for TEXAS BABY,
available September 11, 2007,
as well as other fantastic
Superromance titles
available in September.*

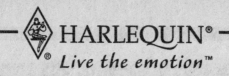

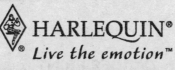

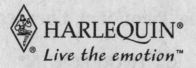

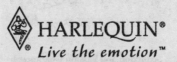

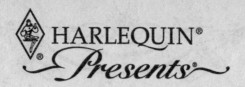

Harlequin® Historical
Historical Romantic Adventure!

*Imagine a time of chivalrous
knights and unconventional ladies,
roguish rakes and impetuous
heiresses, rugged cowboys
and spirited frontierswomen—
these rich and vivid tales will
capture your imagination!*

*Harlequin Historical . . .
they're too good to miss!*

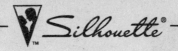

✔ *Silhouette*®
SPECIAL EDITION™

Emotional, compelling stories that capture the intensity of living, loving and creating a family in today's world.

Modern, passionate reads that are powerful and provocative.

✔ *Silhouette*®
nocturne

Dramatic and sensual tales of paranormal romance.

Romances that are sparked by danger and fueled by passion.